# SNATCHED!

# SNATCHED!

GRAHAM MARKS

USBORNE

First published in the UK in 2006 by Usborne Publishing Ltd.,
Usborne House, 83-85 Saffron Hill, London EC1N 8RT, England. www.usborne.com



Illustrations by Philip Bannister.



A CIP catalogue record for this book is available from
the British Library.

JFM MJJASOND/06
ISBN 978 0 7460 6840 3
Printed in India.

# CONTENTS

This one's for Ali and Tony Brown –
the kind of readers a writer loves to have.

My thanks must also go to Megan and Rebecca
for being such a pleasure to work with,
and to Karen Wallace, for her generosity of spirit.

# PROLOGUE

## SMITHFIELD, LONDON
## SEPTEMBER 2ND 1843

The night's storm was over, as quick and angry as a torrential late-summer downpour can sometimes be. It had left the air cooler and smelling like a wet dog, the ground waterlogged. The ragged encampment slowly came back to life, caravan doors opening, spilling out flickering lamplight and tired voices; no one in Hubble's Circus had slept well, the hammering rain, the lightning and the thunder that sounded like the world was coming to an end had seen to that.

Animals clawed nervously at their cages and a lone dog set up a howl at the moon that had appeared through the ragged, scudding clouds; soaked canvas flapped and mud tried to suck the boots from the feet of the sleepy riggers who'd roused themselves to check the ill-lit site for any damage, now that it was no longer raining.

In the calm, the sound of a crying baby stopped everyone in their tracks.

The tiny voice bleated again, echoing in the silence. There were no babies in Hubble's Circus, a fair few children but no babies; there were no women, married or not, ready to give birth, and the crying infant – for it couldn't be anything else – grabbed everyone's attention.

Men checking ropes strained to work out where it came from, people opened caravan windows and others came out onto rickety wooden steps to listen, waiting to see if their ears had fooled them. Had they really heard a baby cry?

Seconds later there was no doubt they had.

"Find it quick!" someone called out. "If the mite's bin out in that weather it might not last much longer!"

From all across the jumble of tents, cages and caravans, people yelled to each other as they searched, the flickering yellow light from oil lanterns casting huge, staggering shadows as they moved.

The door of the largest, but by no means best-kept caravan swung open. "Damnation!" A huge, burly man appeared, rubbing his eyes and squinting out into the darkness. "What gives now – is one of the beasts loose?"

A young boy, standing nearby in a flickering pool of candlelight, pushed his lank hair out of his eyes. "No sir, Mr. Hubble, sir."

"What then?"

"Me mam says there's a baby and we got to find it...case it dies, Mr. Hubble, sir."

"A baby?" Hubble lumbered down his steps. "Whose?"

"Dunno, sir," the boy sniffed, wiping his nose on one of his sleeves. "Not mine..."

"My life I should 'ope not!" Hubble cuffed the boy lightly. "Don't just stand there – get looking!"

Grunting to himself, Hubble watched the boy go. He stood for a moment, wondering in which direction he should set off, or whether he should just go back up into his caravan and let those who cared enough do the looking. What was it to him if there was some child left crying on a night that would make Noah break into a sweat? He had bigger things to worry about, such as running a circus, which was like being in charge of a small village on wheels – with all the troublesomeness and palaver and hair tearing that could bring.

Hubble looked down at his boots, now as muddy as you'd like, and sighed. If he went back into his caravan now, he'd take the filth with him and have achieved nothing except to get his piece of carpet dirty. Shrugging his big, solid shoulders and scratching the hair under his slightly battered top hat, Hubble sighed again and trudged off into the gloom to see what was what and who this fuss was all about.

As he made his way round the site, a pack of small boys raced past him, covered in mud and obviously more involved in a running battle with friends than a search. They swerved round Hubble and disappeared off into the gathering dawn as a second group, this one armed with handfuls of sticky clay, helter-skeltered round the guy ropes of a tent and nearly ran straight into him.

"So this is how you search for a lost 'un, is it?" Hubble stared down at the urchins. "Well, is it?"

The ringleader, or at least the one pushed furthest forward, put his mud-filled hands behind his back. "No sir, Mr. Hubble, sir."

"Get on with it then."

"What, Mr. Hubble, sir?"

"Anything, as long as it don't mean covering me in mud."

Without waiting to be told a second time, the rabble

filed past Hubble and then darted off in search of their friends. He carried on walking, wondering – if it really was a child everyone was looking for and not some cat – why would anyone choose here and now to abandon it? Mustn't want it dead, or they'd've left it where it'd never be found, but for certain they didn't want it to stay in this neck of the woods. If there was one thing you could bet a sure wager on, it was that a circus always moved on.

All around him he could hear evidence of a disorganized, chaotic search in progress: the shouts and curses of men, the anxious calls of women and the playful shrieks of assorted children. Hubble took out his pocket watch, opening it and holding its scratched glass closer to his face: quarter to four, give or take. He'd wanted an early start today, what with the circus moving on, and it looked like he'd surely got one as it was well before dawn. His train of thought was broken when a cry went up – Billy Jiggs, he was pretty sure – saying that he'd found something.

"Where, Billy?" Hubble bellowed.

"By the lion!" came the shouted reply.

Rounding the corner of a tent and passing between two shuttered wagons, Hubble came to a sudden halt, almost slipping over in the mud. In front of him was the lion's cage, with fading gilt lettering running along the top which read: “*LEO – MIGHTY KING OF ANIMALS*”. It was a proud, if inaccurate, boast, but as few, if any, of their patrons had ever seen a lion before, Hubble knew that even the mangy sod slumped at the back on some straw would amaze them. Then he noticed, in the wavering, smoky lamplight, that the slatted wooden side of the cage was propped open.

“What gives here, Billy?” Hubble walked towards the loose circle of people gathered round his chief rigger, who was the man in charge of putting up and taking down the tent. The crowd parted to let him through.

“It’s a child, Mr. Hubble, sir...a boy,” Billy looked down.

That was when Hubble noticed the rigger was holding what looked like a small bundle of cloth in his arms...a small bundle of cloth from which he could just make out that a tiny hand was poking.

“Not more’n hours old, by the looks of him, sir.” Billy parted the white cotton to show the scrunched and wrinkled face beneath it.

“Was almost Leo’s dinner, an’ all, poor little tiny,” said a slightly hunched figure, whose bald head shone dully in the lamplight.

“What’s that, Comus?” Hubble turned to look at the man.

*"It's a child, Mr. Hubble, sir...a boy."*

"He was *in* the cage, Bruise, all wrapped up like a plum pudden." Comus shook his head; the old clown was the only person in the circus allowed to use James Hubble's nickname – gained from his time spent as a bare-knuckle fighter – straight to his battered face.

"In the cage – how so?" Hubble looked accusingly at the crowd, as if to say it must be the fault of at least one of them.

"You know yourself there's been no proper lock on that cage for months, Bruise." Comus walked over, tapping the loose chain with his clay pipe. He'd known Hubble for too long to be scared, like the others, by his gruff manner. "Someone must've come up here in the middle of that rain burst and snuck the child in the cage – though Lord knows why...or who they were."

"Lucky the cat's not long been fed," said the woman who'd moved to stand next to Billy.

"Luckier he ain't got all his teeth!" added a voice from the crowd, to general amusement.

"You take 'im, Hannah." Billy handed the bundle to his wife. "What's to 'appen to him, sir – will he go to the workhouse in the morning?"

"Never that, man!" Hubble frowned, his battle-scarred face creased with anger. "Damn me, but I'd kill before crossing the threshold of another of those blasted holes ever again!"

Mr. Hubble's temper was legendary, his bark and his bite known to be equally as bad as each other, and as water dripped off canvas and wood, the crowd waited and watched.

Hubble stood stock-still, thinking. Truth be told, he'd not really thought there was a child to be found and hadn't given a second's consideration to what would happen if somebody turned one up. But sending even his worst enemy off to the Hell on Earth that was the workhouse...he could never, as long as he had breath in his body, do that. He'd been there, still bore the scars on his back and the pain in his very soul; he spat on the ground, as if to get the taste of the memories out of his mouth. "He'll go nowhere but with us..."

There was an audible sigh of relief from the gathering. Hubble's gravelly voice sank to almost a whisper, so low some of the people didn't hear what he said. "This is my circus and he'll be our child – no damn workhouse lackey will ever lay a finger on him!"

"Our child, Bruise?" Comus raised his eyebrows as he carefully refilled his pipe, the white clay yellowed with age and use.

Everyone looked from the clown to Hubble and held their breath. Even the baby, who hadn't cried since he'd been found, seemed to be waiting to see what would happen.

Hubble beckoned to Billy Jiggs's wife: "Hannah, c'mere...I want a word."

"Me, sir?"

"You ain't done nothin' wrong, woman," Hubble said, "I just want a favour."

Hannah walked over to him, clutching the bundle of cloths to her. The crowd of riggers and gangers, acrobats, riders, clowns and sleepy-eyed children watched.

"The child needs a mother, Hannah, and there's no way in Heaven nor on Earth I can be that." Hubble wiped his mouth on the back of his hand. "If you'll do the job, I'll pay for his keep...give him my name an' all...what d'you say?"

"You knew my answer before you asked, Mr. Hubble," Hannah smiled up at him; "course I will...my last one's bin gone six months and I still feel it like yesterday; I'll make good and sure this one don't die, I promise. What kind of person could've put the poor little thing in Leo's cage anyway? No mother, I'm certain of that!"

"Like as not we'll never know, Hannah." Hubble patted her shoulder. "Now get the both of you home – and Billy, come and see me before we move off, I'll settle some money on you."

"Right." Billy pulled a lock of hair that hung over his forehead; he knew that, even if there'd been no offer of money, Hannah would've taken the child. The death of little Esther – taken by scarlet fever just the last February, and only a year old – had hit her very hard.

"Comus?" Hubble turned to the old clown. "Fancy a drink and a hand of cards?"

"It'd be my pleasure, Bruise."

The two men set off back to Hubble's caravan, one stout and barrel-like, with a back like a ramrod, the other a gnarled, wiry figure. They looked quite comic, the pair of them; not that anyone in the circus would have dared to laugh.

"D'you think we'll make it onto the roads in good time today, Bruise?" Comus tapped his pipe out on a wheel as they walked.

"No doubt."

"Even with the rains making the ground like a bog?"

"Even with that, Comus." Hubble took his hat off and scratched his head. "We've seen worse, you an' I..."

"Thinking about the child?"

"More about who'd do such a thing." Hubble stopped and looked over to check the eastern horizon for any signs that a salmon-pink dawn might be leaking upwards from it. "That looked like good Egyptian cotton he was wrapped in...he didn't come from no poor family, Comus, mark my words. But why put him in that cage?"

"It was open, Bruise, and probably looked safer than leaving him on a step. In that storm they probably didn't stop to look," nodded Comus. "The child was lucky that Leo can't hardly make mincemeat out of mincemeat."

"Got to wonder why, though, haven't you?" Hubble shook his tangle-haired head.

"As you told Hannah – like as not, we'll never know." Comus started walking again. "So what're you going to call the waif?"

"Only one name that'll do." Hubble let his friend go up the steps into his caravan first.

"And what might that be?"

"What else but Daniel?" Hubble smiled. "Daniel from the lion's den."

## CHAPTER 1

# FIRE ON THE ROAD

Wiltshire, late August, 1855

The road came round the hillside in a slow, lazy curve. A few hundred yards below, in a shallow valley, a river meandered its way towards the sea. Heat haze shimmered the air and nothing else seemed to move. Nothing had the energy. And then a sign of life. Round the bend on the edge of the hill a cloud of dust appeared, and with it, surrounded by it, came the leading wagon of Hubble's Circus.

It was pulled by a pair of dirty brown nags, their

iron-shod hooves plodding rhythmically as they hauled their burden up onto the flat. A second wagon followed and behind that another and then another until the entire circus was snaking its way along the side of the hill, throwing up billows of fine, gritty earth as it moved like some fantastic centipede. Mr. Hubble had made them take the often unmetalled public highways again to avoid paying to travel on the turnpikes; he disliked spending money on anything he didn't have to.

From a vantage point on top of the hill Daniel sat on his horse, Savage, and looked down at the circus. His home was on the move again and that was just the way he liked it; how people lived their whole lives out in just one place was beyond him, something he never even tried to understand.

"Back down the hill?" Daniel leaned forward and patted the beast's silky black coat. Savage's ears twitched and he pulled his great head down, snorting as if to say "yes", and he was rewarded by being urged forwards towards the circus.

Daniel loved the time spent travelling between shows, loved the sense of freedom. When you were on the move, he thought, everything was an adventure and nothing was the same as it had been the day before.

*Nothing was the same.*

That thought kept on repeating itself, returning like

an annoying fly to worry at the back of his mind, and no matter how hard he tried he couldn't ignore it. Something had happened to him, something had changed, and he knew that from now on nothing would ever be the same. And inside he was scared.

Since he was tiny Daniel had had dreams, extraordinarily powerful dreams that sometimes seemed almost more real than life itself. He'd grown used to them, and never mentioned them to Hannah or Billy any more, mainly because he'd soon realized that Hannah in particular became very uneasy when he talked about such things. She was a God-fearing woman who thought strange dreams were the Devil's work. And when it came to seeing things when he was wide awake – like yesterday – well, Daniel had an idea she might be right.

It had been early evening after a day of travelling and Daniel was sitting in the caravan. Billy was away doing something and, while he was attempting to fashion a bird whistle from a piece of wood with the pocket knife he always carried with him, attached to his belt by a length of thin plaited cord, Hannah was using the last of the daylight to do some needlework, sewing a bit of loose gold braid back onto his costume. She'd asked him to go to her sewing box and bring her the cork she stuck all her needles in for safe keeping.

The box was on her bed, one of its two lids open, and she'd said he'd find it "in there somewhere". He'd taken the top tray out and was searching in the one underneath it when he came across something small and quite heavy for its size, wrapped in a piece of white cotton. Without thinking to ask, he'd unwrapped it to find a gold sovereign looking as fresh as the day it had been minted. It was when he'd picked the coin up that the waking dream had started...

*...it was night. Outside the room a storm howled like a pack of feral dogs driven wild by the scent of blood, rain hammering at the windows as if desperate to get in and the wind whistling at a pitch almost too high to hear. Curtains fought with the draughts and candles guttered, casting a sallow, wavering light on the scene unfolding within the four walls.*

*On a wide four-poster bed a woman lay in the grip of childbirth, one moment screaming like the storm outside, the next slumped, bathed in sweat, on her pillows. Around her busied a younger woman, mopping her brow, offering her sips of gin and water and brandy, checking the progress this child, the older woman's seventh, was making into the world to join its three surviving brothers.*

*The door to the room opened as the mother-to-be*

*lurched upwards, spitting out small blasphemies as she was taken by another stab of primal agony. A young girl came in carrying a large china jug...*

Daniel, gasping at the clarity and power of what he'd seen, had dropped the coin like it was burning his fingers, and found himself in his caravan once more. Hannah had looked up to see what the matter was, anxious he might have cut himself. He'd asked her why she kept a sov wrapped up in her sewing box and she called him over to where she was sitting by the door. She'd found the coin when she'd unwrapped him that night twelve years ago, she said, and wrapped it in a piece of the cloth he'd been found in. It was the only past he had, she'd said, and they'd been intending to give it to him on his twenty-first birthday.

Last night he'd lain awake, wondering about what had, or maybe hadn't, occurred. Had he, maybe, simply imagined the whole thing? That in itself was enough of a worry, and the thought had led to a restless night of wondering what the scene had meant, who the people were...and why he'd been abandoned, yet left with so much money?

He didn't often think about being abandoned, mostly because there was always too much else to do, which didn't leave time in the day for thinking; and then, truth be told, he was really quite happy where he was and who he was with. Occasionally, when the circus was pitched near London – and especially when they went back for Bartelmy Fair, because that was when and where he'd been left – he'd find himself wondering who he might have been, and what he might be doing, had his mother not let him go.

On those occasions, in the minutes grabbed between practice and performance, he'd sometimes find himself searching the faces in the thronging crowds, imagining which person might be his mother, his father, his brother, his sister. It could be anyone, though more likely it was none of them, but in those moments, moments when he felt so empty and alone, he wished and wished he knew the truth. Even though he knew what old Comus had once told him – that the truth could hurt – was right.

Lying awake, thinking about the vision he'd seen when he'd picked up the sov, Daniel didn't want to admit to himself, let alone anyone else, that he'd seen something when he'd touched the coin. It was like what Ma Tilley did for the gulls who came to have their fortunes told. Except this was seeing the past, not the future. This was like witchcraft.

And then it had happened again earlier today. Just after dawn.

He'd been out with Billy, seeing to the horses just like he did every day, when he felt the weirdest cold shiver run through him; the hairs on the back of his head bristled, his fingers tingled and the horse he was leading spooked so bad he almost lost hold of the reins.

In front of him he saw the whole bustle of the circus, where seconds before there'd been an empty field. He was right there in the thick of the crowd, standing next to the small spare caravan with a rough, painted wooden sign above the doorway that had the name Rosalie and two roses hand carved on it. It was the new one that Mr. Hubble had recently purchased. Daniel could hear, see and smell what was going on but people walked past him as if he wasn't there. Then a woman looked out of the caravan.

She was pretty, but not beautiful, with long, curly, russet-red hair that shone in the sunlight; she had dark eyes and a wide smile that revealed a couple of gold teeth. Someone called out a name: "Josie!" they shouted...and the woman turned round.

Daniel looked the same way to see who had called and the circus was gone. He was standing in a field in the cool morning light, gripping the reins as if his life depended on it.

"You all right?"

Daniel looked behind him and saw Billy, an old

leather bucket in one hand and his stick in the other, staring at him. "What?" he said.

"Something up?" Billy limped towards him; five years previously Billy had fallen, through someone else's error, while the trapeze was being put up and had broken his leg. Hannah had done her best to set it, but Billy would never walk straight again. "You look like you seen a ghost, boy."

Daniel shook his head. "Who's Josie, Billy?" He said it without thinking, looking back over his shoulder at where he'd seen the red-headed woman.

"Where'd you hear that name?" Billy whispered, his eyes darting about, checking they were alone. "Who's been talking?"

"No one, Billy," Daniel frowned, "I just saw...I, uh, I just heard it."

"Well keep it to yerself and don't repeat it." Billy pointed his stick at him. "She's someone that's joining us at Marlborough, friend of Mr. Hubble's. It's s'posed to be a secret...now let's get the work done, lad."

Daniel nodded. He felt totally confused – why was Billy so concerned that he'd known the name of Mr. Hubble's friend? What had he seen this time...the future? And, if that was true, what on earth was happening to him?

* * *

Even now, hours later, Daniel had no answers to anything. The whole circus was rife with rumours about the person they were meeting at Marlborough – so much for Billy's secret – although there were as many theories as to who it was and why it was a secret as there were people talking.

Daniel touched Savage lightly with his willow switch, urging him to go even faster; gripping hard with his knees, holding tight onto the silky black mane, boy and horse sped across the wide swathe of green towards the rumbling, dusty circus. It felt, thought Daniel, almost as if he was flying, as if Savage had wings like the horse in a story Comus liked to tell him. Only that horse's name was Pegasus and, according to Comus, he'd been born when this man, Perseus, had cut the head off a woman called Medusa who had snakes for hair. Comus knew hundreds of these tall tales.

As he leaned over to his right, Savage instantly picking up the signal and turning, Daniel's mind thought back to the morning; what was really getting to him was that he hadn't been able to say anything to anyone about his experience. It had been on his mind the whole day and people kept on asking him if they could pay a penny for his thoughts. They could pay a whole guinea and they still wouldn't learn very much because he didn't know *what* to think.

He rode beside the cavalcade of wagons, hardly paying them any attention, even the wheeled lion's cage – the very one he'd been found in – where the same lion, twelve years older now and truly on his last legs, lay slumped and panting in the heat.

Overtaking the dusty column, Daniel pulled hard on the reins and took Savage off the road again and down towards the glinting river. As he did so, two other riders broke away from the wagons and came after him on their horses. Spotting the movement, Daniel squinted over his shoulder and made out that it was Jem and Seth, who were apprentice riggers working with Billy, and his two best friends in the whole world. They'd recently become blood brothers, cutting their thumbs in a secret ceremony one day a few weeks back and holding them together as they all whispered, "*For ever!*"

Daniel knew the boys wanted a race, but there was no way they'd catch him up, Savage was the fastest horse in the circus and Daniel was the best rider, even bareback like he was now. He'd ridden almost since the day he could walk and was now one of the main attractions of Hubble's Circus. His friends were good, but their horses were nags in comparison to Savage and their skills were with ropes, not riding. He beat Jem and Seth to the river's edge with yards to spare.

"Ain't seen much of you today, Dan." Jem slipped to

the ground as Seth reined in his sweating horse close by.

"Been around." Daniel led Savage down into the water so he could drink.

Seth followed him with his horse. "You heard about that woman's coming down to Marlborough, Dan?" Daniel nodded. "Bet you didn't know it was Bruise's wife, now did you!"

"Sticky Jack told me she was some new act – dances on the ropes, something like that." Jem brought his own horse to join them at the water's edge.

"Well Sticky's got porridge for brains!" Seth kicked water at his friend and got a handful back in reply.

Daniel wasn't paying attention. Deep in the back of his mind he could feel a strange sensation and for a moment he couldn't think why it scared him. And then he realized it was the same feeling he'd had in the field that morning...

He suddenly felt very cold. Seth and Jem's voices faded into the background and his eyes lost their ability to focus. Daniel could hear a dull, echoing thump in his ears, the beat getting louder and louder, and for a moment he thought he might be dying. He wanted to say something, shout for his two companions to help him, but his voice wouldn't work.

And then he saw it. Fire.

From out of the misty blur in front of him came sheets of flame, and with them the sounds of terrified animals and screaming people. The noises echoed and boomed, like voices in a tunnel; he could smell burning and the colours in the fire were vibrant; the flames leaped and danced, alive like children chasing round a Maypole. It was almost pretty.

Daniel was rigid with fear, even though part of him knew what he was seeing wasn't actually happening and that, if he could make himself walk into the fire, he wouldn't burst into flames. Not like the straw bales he could see, the ones the woman who looked like Sticky Jack's wife, holding up her skirts and petticoats, was trying to put out with a sodden blanket. He could feel the panic rising in his chest, making it difficult for him to breathe; he wanted to shout out, to do something that would end the terrible sights in front of him, but that was the one thing he couldn't do.

Thoughts flickered through his head like the flames in front of him – was he ill, had he caught some disease in his head that made him see dreams, nightmares even, when he was awake? Was he awake? Just because he'd been right about the name of Mr. Hubble's mysterious friend didn't mean everything he saw was true. Did it?

Daniel knew, somehow, that what he was seeing was

different from a dream, that it was more than his imagination playing tricks; he could feel it, feel that what he saw was possible and that his whole world could be destroyed, and everyone he knew and cared for put in jeopardy. It couldn't be going to happen, it mustn't happen!

His head felt like it was about to explode. The enormity of what he was seeing, his total inability to do anything – even close his eyes and stop seeing it – was bad enough, but the thought that it might actually happen took the breath right out of him. He couldn't bear the idea that he was watching harm come to the people who'd found him, loved him and given him a life, and the biggest, most extraordinary family it was possible to imagine. He could not lose all that!

Only then did he find his voice, and he screamed...

The piercing wail of his own tortured voice jolted him out of the nightmare vision and Daniel staggered backwards. His eyes were full of hot, salty tears and for a second he had no idea where he was...he could hear someone calling his name, could hear the whinnying and stamping of horses and his own deep sobbing.

"No!" Daniel cried out, and as he brought his hands up to his face he tripped on a rock. He heard Jem's muffled yell of "Catch him!", and then he was underwater.

The icy coldness cut like a newly-stropped razor and when he took a sharp breath it wasn't air that filled his lungs. He felt hands frantically grabbing for him and then, coughing and spluttering, he was dumped on his face in the long grass by the river bank.

Jem kneeled down beside Daniel. "Is he dead, Seth?"

"Not till he stops hackin' his guts up he's not." Seth thumped Daniel's back with the flat of his hand.

"What shall I do?"

"Make sure as the horses don't take to their heels, for a start," Seth whacked Daniel again, "and then help me get Dan back on his feet."

As Daniel lay in the grass, fighting for breath, just the smallest one would do, the pictures and sounds of blazing canvas and terrified animals came flooding back – had he really seen something that was going to happen?

He wouldn't know, until they got to Marlborough, whether the red-headed woman he'd seen looked like the person supposedly coming to meet them, but if she did...if she did, then would that mean a terrible fire would destroy the circus?

And would anyone believe him if he tried to warn them?

# CHAPTER 2
# COMUS

Unfortunately, Hannah had caught wind of the fact that Daniel had had what she insisted on calling "a turn", and even though he felt fine, he hadn't managed to convince her there was nothing the matter with him after that. Much to Seth and Jem's amusement she'd insisted he take a rest in the caravan. For an orphan, he thought, and not for the first time, he was a very lucky person.

As soon as things calmed down and Hannah had stopped fretting and treating him like he was ill, Daniel escaped back out into the world again, the world of animals and acrobats and tumblers and fortune-tellers. It was a world that was as real to him as any street in any town or village they passed through was to those who lived there; but, he knew to outsiders this was a magical and dangerous place, full of the freakish, the weird and the wonderful.

What the people who came never realized was that a lot of what they saw at the circus was what they wanted to see, wanted to believe in. When Mr. Hubble did his patter and told people that, when he drew back the curtain, they were going to be truly and indisputably amazed by *Mr. Walking Stick – Absolutely and Without Doubt the Thinnest Man in the Whole of This Very Wide World!* that's what they saw. True, Sticky Jack – dressed up in his tall, tall hat and tight white suit with the vertical black stripes, lamplight shining up at him to accentuate his cheekbones – really did look much like a strong draught could blow him over, but it still amazed Daniel how gullible and trusting some folk were.

Not much was what it seemed in a travelling show, but then they never stayed anywhere long enough for that to matter too much; even Daniel wasn't who the audience thought he was. With his long, jet-black hair, greased-back into a ponytail, and dressed up in a red, military-style uniform, when he rode Savage out into the ring it was as *Crown Prince Juan Pablo of Nicobar – the Youngest Equestrian Master in This, or Any Other, Hemisphere – on Ozymandias, his Magnificent Arab Stallion!*

He had no idea where in the world Nicobar was, but he had to admit that, dressed in his costume, sitting astride Savage and waiting for the ringmaster's introduction to finish with a mighty crack of his whip, he was glad he wasn't going out as plain Daniel Hubble. By the time he appeared, his audiences were all ready for an exotic spectacle of riding skills, and that's exactly what they got. He might've been born in London – and Savage was no more an Arab stallion than he was a chicken – but no one went away from Hubble's Circus without having seen a show they'd always remember.

As darkness fell, and lamps were lit, Daniel began to wander through the temporary site. It was home because of who was there, not where they were. In that respect, anywhere was home, anywhere at all, as long as he was with these people.

Daniel's throat was still a bit sore from coughing up all the water he'd swallowed and his back felt bruised from Seth's doctoring thumps, but he was alive. It was when he tried to think about what he'd seen – and more, what to do about it – that Daniel had real problems. The circus had stopped for the night by the side of the road they'd been travelling on, and as Daniel wandered through the untidy collection of wagons he started to try and gather his thoughts.

Who should he talk to? Would Mr. Hubble understand what had happened? He thought probably not; his benefactor was a man who saw the world as a place where you had to fight with your bare hands to stay afloat. Kind and generous though he was – he had, after all, given Daniel his name and called him his son – he had no time for what he'd no doubt think of as flights of fancy. Then there were Hannah and Billy Jiggs. Hannah would, like as not, have him straight off to the nearest priest if he said anything to her, and Billy would just look embarrassed and want to be somewhere else.

Which, of all the people in the circus, left Comus.

Daniel knew in his heart the old clown was the most likely person to take him seriously. He'd listened for hours on end to Comus's stories, tales of his adventures in outlandish and mysterious foreign parts that often changed with every telling, but still managed to have a ring of truth about them. The only thing stopping Daniel from going straight to the old clown's caravan was the fact that he felt bad about burdening someone else with the knowledge, if you could call it that, of what he'd seen; what he believed was going to happen. But if anyone would have an open mind, Comus would.

"Well," Daniel said to himself out loud, "Comus it's got to be..."

"Fust sign a madness, boy," a deep voice rumbled above him, "talking to yo'self."

Daniel was standing near a caravan he'd thought was empty, and the voice that came out of the darkness made him jump. "That you, Sam?" He peered through the open door. But Sam Baston was blacker than road pitch and Daniel couldn't make him out.

"Ain't got a twin, so prob'ly it must be." Sam appeared in the doorway, a huge, bald giant, the biggest man Daniel had ever seen, with a strongman act billed as *Baron Magnus, the Mighty Ox* – Mr. Hubble being very partial to the word "mighty". "How ya been after the swim, Dan?"

"I'm fine." Daniel smiled up at the man from the Indies, whose slow, drawn-out accent he'd never lost his fascination for.

"Ya look a mite worried...sometin' on ya mind, boy?"

"Yes..." said Daniel.

"Well you best get off an' see Comus, then." Sam's eyes looked to his left and Daniel saw a flash of white. "He got a *fine* set a ears, that man – but come by later,

Dan, I'm makin' a good stew, rabbit an' stuff, if ya'd like some."

"I will, Sam...and thanks." Daniel smiled, waved and then left to find the only person who might be able to help him.

"Seeing things?" Comus took a pinch of snuff out of the small silver box that, along with his clay pipe and leather tobacco pouch, he always carried with him.

"Not saints or anything, Comus." Daniel watched the man's thin, spider-like fingers put a tiny pile of brown powder on his fisted left hand and sniff it up his right nostril. He'd found Comus napping in his caravan and had been about to go away when the old man had woken up and called him back.

"What was it then?" Comus repeated the ritual Daniel had seen him do a thousand or more times, taking some snuff up his right nostril, then sneezing loudly and blowing his nose on a grimy rag.

Daniel took a deep breath and told Comus everything in as much detail as he could muster, watching him as he just sat and listened, still and silent as if he was made of wood. When he'd finished, Daniel half expected Comus to burst out laughing, or maybe tell him angrily he was talking nonsense. Instead, he blew his nose again, then stuffed his pipe, struck a lucifer on a boot nail and lit the bowl with agonizing slowness, all as if nothing at all had been said.

"Do you believe me?" Daniel watched a cloud of acrid smoke waft up to the caravan's roof.

"You've always told the truth before," Comus sucked on the pipe's dark brown stem, "so I've no reason not to...it's a fine tangle of a story, Daniel my boy, what with the then and the now all being mixed together, and no one wants to hear about fire in business like ours. Truthfully, I wouldn't know *what* to make of any of it, really I wouldn't, 'cept it sounds to me like you're describing Josie Finnister to a likeness."

"I am? Who is she?"

"Last time I saw her she was a slip of a girl, though," Comus puffed a couple of times, "no gold teeth or nothing."

"So who is she?"

"She's the person we're meeting."

"Mr. Hubble's wife?"

Comus laughed, coughed and then spat out of his window. "That what they've bin saying?" Daniel nodded and Comus shook his head, still laughing. "Lord, but can you imagine old Bruise ever getting wed? The woman ain't been born would want to take that job on!"

"They not friends then?"

"No, not friends, as such." Comus tamped down the

bowl of his pipe. "Years back, her father and Bruise, when they were young and full of piss 'n' vinegar, they were the finest bare-knuckle men anywhere. Types used to come to London from all over to fight those boys. It was before the circus, but I knew of them both. Everyone did."

"Why's she coming here...why's it such a big secret?"

"Couldn't tell you, boy, and wouldn't if I could. Not my business, and won't be until the man thinks it right that I know."

Daniel felt like he'd been very gently put in his place. He looked at Comus. "What about...you know?" he asked.

"What you saw?"

Daniel nodded.

Comus wiped his nose on the back of his hand. "I could say go away and stop your worrying, but that would do no one no good; I could say a lot of things, but I need to have a think first, to do the problem justice."

"You think it's a problem?"

"I'm not saying anything for now, Daniel." Comus stood up. "You go and get to your bed...early start tomorrow, early start, like always...we'll have a talk tomorrow, boy, a good one."

# CHAPTER 3
# WAITING FOR JOSIE FINNISTER

The next day seemed to Daniel to be the longest in his life. Nothing different happened; he still got up before dawn, woken, as usual, by Hannah gently stroking his cheek; after a tin mug of sweet tea, with a chunk of yesterday's bread to dip in it, he, like everyone else, got down to the job of readying the circus for the day ahead. They had to be at their destination in time to pitch and put on a performance that night. Everything just as usual, no time to think of anything but the job in hand. But the minutes seemed to go by as if they were hours and the hours passed with the slowness of livelong days, time dragging its heels like it was walking in molasses.

They were moving well before five, the sun just beginning its crawl up over the pink horizon, but once on the road it was no better. Normally there would be a four-, maybe five-hour journey ahead but today, of all days, everything went wrong: a wheel broke, a couple of horses lost shoes, a child went missing. Each event halted the circus for however long it took to sort out and Daniel thought they'd be stuck between Here and There for ever, maybe longer.

And the worst of it was that all this time allowed him to think about things he'd rather not. He didn't want to have waking dreams, he didn't want to see events that were possibly going to happen. He didn't want any of it. What he did want was to meet this Josie Finnister and see just how much like the person he'd seen she was, and then he wanted to sit down with Comus again and talk everything through with him. Comus was the oldest, wisest person he knew. He was bound to know the answers to all the questions Daniel felt were chasing him like dogs after a hare.

Apart from the stopping and starting it was an easy journey and, as he rode Savage up and down the long line of wagons, he kept his mind free of unwanted thoughts by surprising any of the drivers he found had fallen asleep, reins hanging loosely in their hands as the draught horses plodded rhythmically along in front of them.

Just before nine they passed Barbury Castle, away up on a hill, and Daniel knew they were only a very slow couple of miles or so from their destination: Marlborough. Josie Finnister might even be there now if she'd taken the train and not come by stage, and Daniel wondered how much longer he'd have to wait till he finally saw her. And find out if she truly was the person he'd seen. If she was, would that mean the fire was really going to happen?

Normally, around this time of year, Daniel could only ever think of one thing: his birthday was in a couple of days' time – or, more precisely, the anniversary of the night he arrived at the circus – and there was always a big party after the last performance. September 2nd, in Hubble's Circus at least, was known as Daniel's Day and it was without doubt the best day of the year for Daniel. But now his mind was elsewhere, thinking dark thoughts about whether there'd even be a Hubble's Circus next year or just ashes and memories.

"Danny! Danny!"

Daniel snapped out of his bad daydream and saw

Jem, swiftly followed by Seth, gallop past him. "What?" he yelled back, Savage responding instantly to his light heel kicks.

"Mr. Hubble wants us to go ahead and see to it that the posters the advance man put up are still there!" Seth slowed down, shouting over his shoulder, then urged his horse to a gallop.

A race was on and all thoughts of anything else but catching up his friends – and then beating them to the first poster – vanished like the morning mist. Daniel could see Jem had a satchel slung over his back, which he knew would have spare posters, a couple of hammers and some nails in it, but all that mattered right then was narrowing the distance between him and his friends.

It wasn't going to be easy, as both Seth and Jem had saddled up and he was riding bareback, but Savage was fast and Daniel didn't need any saddle to stay stuck on his back like he was glued down. He wanted to win and he knew Savage wanted to win as well. Daniel could feel the same need for victory in the horse, in the way the beautiful creature lengthened his stride, responded to the smallest, lightest touch and seemed to have infinite speed within him. Holding onto Savage's coarse but lustrous mane, Daniel didn't have to do anything but will his mount on, and seconds later he was thundering past first Seth and then Jem, as both boys urged their horses to go faster still. And failed.

Rounding a bend in the road, a hundred or so yards away Daniel could see a large piece of white paper tacked to a tree; there was printing on it, too far away to read, but it looked like one of their posters and he was sure the words on it would say:

**HUBBLE'S MAGNIFICENT CIRCUS**

**THE PROPRIETOR RESPECTFULLY**
**INFORMS THE GOOD PEOPLE HEREABOUTS**
**THAT THERE WILL SOON BE ARRIVING:**
**ACROBATS, EQUESTRIANS & ANIMALS,**
**CLOWNS, ODDITIES & STRONGMEN**
**MANY & VARIOUS EXTRAORDINARY ACTS**
**FROM ALL OVER THE KNOWN WORLD**

**FOR YOUR ENTERTAINMENT!**

With one final burst of speed Savage took Daniel past the tree at full gallop and then, the race won, slowed to a trot as he felt the tension leave his rider.

"How's he do it, Danny boy?" Seth pulled his horse

up beside Savage as Jem trotted past them both. "He don't even look like he was tryin'."

"Don't know, and I don't care," Daniel smiled, patting Savage's smooth neck, "so long as he keeps on doing it."

"Come on you two, we got posters to check!" Jem moved off down the road at a canter.

"Once we done the posters, Mr. Hubble said as how he wants us to get to the field, start collecting wood for the fires." Seth tapped his horse with the willow switch he was carrying. "And we got to keep our eyes peeled for that lady...you know, the one what ain't his wife?"

"Josie Finnister."

Seth nodded. "That's her name."

"Why've we got to look out for her?"

"Mr. Hubble says she could be arriving at the field before he gets there and he don't want her to be there on her own, or have to go back into the town or anything."

"Right."

Seth looked over at Daniel. "Who d'you think she is, then?"

"Her father knew Mr. Hubble...back when he was fighting."

"How'd you get to know that?"

"I asked Comus yesterday, and he told me so."

"He say anything else?"

"Only that it was none of anyone's business, until Mr. Hubble told them."

"I bet he knows more'n he's saying," Seth grinned and winked at Daniel. "Those two, they're as thick as them thieves in the rookeries down Seven Dials and St Giles."

"They've known each other a long time, nothing more than that, Seth. That's all."

Daniel could see that his tone of voice had made Seth realize he may have gone too far. While Daniel lived with Billy and Hannah, who were like his mother and father, it was best to remember it was Mr. Hubble himself who'd given him his names. He was Daniel Hubble, not Daniel Jiggs.

"Didn't mean nothing, right?" Seth punched his friend's arm.

Nodding, Daniel took the apology silently. He never forgot that in truth he had three people who thought they were responsible for him, though others often did; people always had things to say and opinions about the big man they worked for, and they were rarely what a kind, honest, upstanding-type he was. Daniel knew James Hubble was a hard man, but then he'd slogged his way up a hard path to get to where he was and, no matter what, he was fair to those loyal to him. And in this life, as Billy Jiggs always said, that was about as good as it got.

The three boys had ridden through the town, where it looked like Howie Martin, the advance man, who'd been through maybe ten days, two weeks before, had done a pretty fair job. Most of the posters were still where he'd pasted them and they'd only had to put up a couple of new ones where someone had taken them down.

That job done they'd got themselves over to the field where the circus would pitch for the night's show, tethered the horses to a hedgerow and started gathering wood and piling it up in the corner where the sod would be taken up, pits dug and fires lit to cook the breakfast everyone had been waiting for since they'd rolled out of bed before dawn. Daniel could almost smell the bacon now and his stomach growled like Sticky Jack's dog. Tomorrow morning the pits would be filled back in, the sod put back on and you'd hardly know they'd ever been dug.

Dropping an armful of fallen branches onto the growing pile, Seth squinted up at the clear sky. "I'd say it's likely close to eleven o'clock." He wiped sweat out of his eyes with his sleeve. "They should be here any time now, right Jem?"

"'Less something else's happened on the way."

"Already had three things today." Daniel arrived with his load of firewood. "Nothing else should go wrong now."

"What three?" Jem frowned.

"The broken wheel, those two horses losing a shoe," Daniel counted on his fingers, "and all that fuss when they couldn't find that little girl."

"Old wives' tale, that, things going in threes."

Seth picked a long blade of grass and started chewing it. "My mother says it's true they do that, go in threes."

"Like I said," Jem nodded, grinning, "old wife's tale!"

"Oi!" Seth picked up a large stick and lobbed it. "My mam ent old!" Jem, who'd been expecting just such a response, caught the piece of wood and ran off.

Daniel hunkered down and picked himself a stem of grass to chew on. "How much more wood d'you two think we need?" he called out, watching Seth chase Jem around the pile of branches.

Jem ran in front of Daniel and stopped, using him as a barrier. "I'd say we'd better get some more – they'll only complain if there's not enough and as soon as the wagons arrive we'll have more work..." he waved the branch at Seth, "...than you can shake a stick at!"

* * *

By the time the lead wagon appeared at the end of the lane, half an hour later, the three boys had collected a heap of wood almost taller than themselves and they were resting in what little shade was cast by a scrubby old hawthorn tree.

The arrival of the circus was like watching a garden grow, especially as the tents went up, the canvas unfolding like flower petals. Wagons were unpacked, ropes uncoiled and slowly the garden blossomed. Everything had a pattern, everything had its place and everyone their job to do to make ready for the performance.

By now the whole town would know the circus had arrived; if they hadn't been there to watch the colourful, noisy procession through the middle of town, people would've heard about it from someone who was. Hubble's was by no means the biggest of the circuses out on the roads, but they had a reputation for being honest travellers with a good show and reasonable prices.

Seth, Jem and Daniel were getting ready to start working – Daniel with Billy, feeding and grooming the horses, Jem and Seth with their fathers, who were both gangers, setting up the tents and stalls – when Mr. Hubble steered his wagon out of the line and pulled up next to them.

He looked over at the pile of wood and nodded. "Good job there, boys, good job."

"Thank you, Mr. Hubble, sir," Seth answered for all of them.

"No sign of anyone, then?"

"No, sir, not since we bin here. No one arrived."

Mr. Hubble looked at each boy in turn, like he was calculating their worth and value, then he nodded again. "Jem, get yerself down to the town...see if the lady in question has got herself up from Pewsey."

"Pewsey, Mr. Hubble, sir?" Jem frowned.

"She's coming down by train...nearest stop to Marlborough's Pewsey; tell your father I need you to do me an errand." He tapped the horses onward, looking over his shoulder as the wagon moved. "And come and find me soon as you get back."

Seth watched Jem, grinning from ear to ear, get on his horse. "How come you get the slacker's job then?"

"Don't ask me." Jem slapped his mount's haunch and took off at a gallop.

"Is that fair?" Seth looked to Daniel, shrugging.

"He'll likely miss breakfast."

"So he will, Danny-boy, so he will!" Seth slapped Daniel's shoulder. "We'll have his – tell the cooks we're saving it for him till he gets back, and then split it between us. That'll teach him to get chosen for the easy life!"

As the two boys walked off, following their noses to the cooking pits, Daniel felt more than hunger in his gut. There was a nervousness as well, a sense of anticipation. Exactly who was it coming down from London? And why...?

## CHAPTER 4

# THE FIRST SIGHT

Daniel was cleaning the last of the road dust off the last horse, with one eye on the pile of harnesses and such that needed all its leather and brass polishing, when word came by that "the woman" had arrived.

He wanted to drop his curry-comb and go right away to see her, but he knew he shouldn't and he couldn't. Not while there was work to do. Not while Hannah was repairing costumes, Billy was mixing feed and from all over the field he could hear the sounds of other people's labours. Sledgehammers thundered on stakes as long as a man's outstretched arms, there was the rhythmical call of gangs hauling up the main tent and the flap of canvas being unfolded. No one had the time to go looking and staring at strangers, least of all him. After finishing the horses and the tackle, Savage had to be taken to the smithy to have his shoes done and then he'd be out with Billy, going over the routines, doing what they called "sharpening up the show". It was while Jack Banner, the smithy, was dealing with Savage that Daniel realized he finally had time that he could call his own.

"Jack?"

"Daniel?" The smithy looked up as he pulled nails out of one of Savage's front hooves.

"All right if I nip off for a moment...you need me here for anything?"

"Not as I can see, less you think you can make a better shoe'n me. I'll be finished with the boy," he patted Savage's side, "in, I should say, ooh, less than half an hour?"

"I'll be here before then, Jack."

It was his guess that Josie Finnister would be with Mr. Hubble, and as he ran through the bustling campsite, looking for the big man's distinctive red and green caravan, Daniel tried to look like he was on an errand in case anyone thought to give him another job.

And then there it was.

Daniel stopped, realizing that he hadn't thought out what he should do next; he watched the thin, twisting snake of smoke escape from the caravan's chimney, smelled its sharp, aromatic scent; he saw that although the curtains were roughly pulled on the window, the door was open. He could sidle up and see if he could hear whatever it was they were talking about inside, though he'd never want to get caught doing that. So maybe he should just walk by and hope Mr. Hubble saw him. If he did, maybe he'd call him in and introduce him. Or...he couldn't think of anything else to do except go up the steps, knock on the side of the caravan and ask if he could come in.

"Are you Daniel?"

Daniel jerked round. "Ye..."

The word stuck in his throat, almost like he'd choked on it. He was looking up at a pretty, dark-eyed, red-headed woman, who, when she smiled, he could see had two gold teeth.

"Cat got your tongue?"

Daniel glanced away. Just as Comus had said the night before, he'd seen Josie Finnister and described her to a likeness. And now here she was, standing there, talking to him. How he wished he'd been able to speak to the old clown, find out what he thought was happening to him, but he hadn't and right now the lady in question was looking quizzically at him and he had to say something...

"No, ma'am."

"Would that be, no, you're not Daniel, or no, the cat ain't got your tongue?"

"I'm Daniel," he glanced up, pushing a thick lock of hair out of his eyes. "Pleased to meet you, miss, I mean, ma'am."

"Josie will do." The woman looked him up and down and made Daniel feel like he was something on sale in a market. "So, you're Daniel...Bruise told me about you – maybe I should have called you Crown Prince Juan Pablo." She dipped a small, not very serious curtsey.

Daniel nodded, forcing a smile onto his face as he didn't know what to think of this woman and wasn't sure he liked her. What he was sure of was that she looked *exactly* as he'd seen in his head and he was almost shocked by how accurate his picture of her had been. Except for the fact that she was dressed differently in a long, dark-green skirt of a velvety material and a similar coloured jacket trimmed with some kind of dark-brown fur at the neck and wrists – and her thick red hair was pulled back away from her face and pinned up – she was the mirror image of the woman he'd seen in that strange, waking dream.

"So you two've met, then."

Daniel looked behind him to see Mr. Hubble standing in the doorway of his caravan. You could never tell what mood he was in by his expression; his battered face never giving anything away, but he sounded if not exactly happy, then not unhappy.

"He's a mite shy, Bruise."

"Dazzled by yer beauty, more like."

Daniel could feel himself blushing and wanted nothing more than to get back to the smithy's where the only reason he'd be red-faced would be because of the heat of the white-hot coals.

"You got yerself nothing to do, Daniel?"

"I'm waiting for Savage to be shod, then I'm off to practise with Billy, sir."

"Well come inside, have a quick mug of tea and meet Josie properly; I've got a pot brewed." Hubble turned, then looked over his shoulder at Daniel still standing where he was. "Get a move on, son."

Daniel didn't often get to come into this caravan. He might carry Mr. Hubble's surname, but this wasn't his home and, truth be known, Billy Jiggs was the person he thought of as his father. And he was beginning to think it was about time he got back to collect Savage.

He sat near the door half-watching Mr. Hubble and this newcomer, Josie, and wondering what her connection with the big man was. She didn't look like the other women in the circus – certainly nothing like Hannah; for a start there looked to be powder on her face and colour on her lips and cheeks, and Daniel was sure he could smell a lavender scent. Not something you'd ever think of finding in Mr. Hubble's caravan.

Daniel was used to the way people treated Mr. Hubble, with a respect verging on awe (and that was when he was in a good mood), and here was this woman – who looked quite young, her fair, freckled skin unlined – seemingly treating him as a friend. Almost an equal! Daniel was fascinated by her, the way she was, who she might be, why she was here at all.

"I shall look forward to seeing your act tonight, Daniel."

Daniel, who'd been staring into the middle distance, thinking, jumped and looked up at Josie as she took a chipped enamel mug from Mr. Hubble. "Um...thank you, ma'am," he said as she blew on its steaming contents.

"I haven't seen Josie since she was about your age, Daniel." Hubble handed another mug to Daniel and then sat down and began cleaning out the bowl of his pipe with a small pocket knife. "Her dad an' me, we used to have some fun, didn't we, girl?"

"If you call getting yourselves beat till your faces looked like a piece of beef, then that's true, Bruise."

Hubble inspected his scarred knuckles. "Morgan was a good man, a good man and a good friend. I'm sorry I wasn't there when he lost The Sun, or round very much for you after he died and you was left without much more'n a job at the tavern. This place..."

"I know, Bruise...but you did what you could and you're helping me now, when I *really* need it. If Carter Bland's people ever find me there'll be the very Devil to pay!" Josie looked pale and worry lines creased her forehead. "He'll stop at nothing to get it back, Bruise, and I *wish* I hadn't taken it..."

Daniel felt like he was intruding, and something told him he was party to a conversation he possibly shouldn't be hearing; the look on Mr. Hubble's face confirmed he was right.

"Daniel?"

"Yessir?"

"You listen up, now." Hubble leaned forward and looked Daniel straight in the eye. "You shouldn't a'heard this, as I think you must've realized, but now that you have you should know it's very possible there are some rapscallions out looking fer Josie. They want something they *think* what she's got with her, see. But she *ain't* got it as it's still up in the Smoke, right?"

Daniel nodded again, hardly believing Mr. Hubble was taking him into his confidence, although he had no idea what he was being told really meant.

"No need for this to go any further, but I'm going to need some help from you, and the likes of Jem an' Seth."

Daniel glanced at Josie and then back at Mr. Hubble. "What can we do?"

"Tell the rest that I heard some ruffians might be trying to make a bit of trouble for us, an' they're to keep their eyes well peeled for any strangers hanging round the camp." Hubble dug into one of his waistcoat pockets and flicked a small silver coin over towards Daniel, who grabbed the flying sixpenny piece out of the air. "That's all you tell 'em, mind."

"Yessir!"

"Now you better go to your work, or Billy'll have yer guts fer garters."

Billy was not best pleased with Daniel's practise in the ring. He'd made a couple of stupid mistakes, mistakes he knew could have left him badly hurt, because his mind was elsewhere, thinking about his meeting with Josie and what she could possibly have left up in London that would make her need to come and hide out with them. So, because he wasn't concentrating, Billy was making him go over everything a couple more times, just to make sure, which meant that he hadn't had a chance to find Seth or Jem or anyone to tell them what Mr. Hubble wanted them to do.

"Think, Danny, Savage can't do it all for you!" Billy stood in the middle of the ring, watching every move Daniel made as he raced round in a tight circle, now with two horses – one foot on Savage's back, the other on a white mare called Snowdrop.

As Daniel came round he saw one of the riggers swing out a hoop and he readied himself for the leap forward and mid-air somersault that would take him through the steel band and down onto Savage. During the show the hoop would be *A Veritable Flaming Ring of Fire!* as it would be covered in lit spirit-soaked rags and he would go through it twice, landing once on each horse.

He gave the whistled signal and beneath him he could feel the horses slow down slightly so that they'd be in the right place for him to land. Tensing, he jumped, like he was about to dive into a pond, and threw himself forward, his world turning as he tucked his head down and rolled through the air. As his feet came down and his shoulders span upwards he flung his arms out and then there he was, feet on solid horse again. A perfect landing.

"Good...good, Danny...that's fine."

Yes, it was fine, but Daniel hated getting things wrong and the showman in him had to prove that he was better than good. He knew Billy meant he could stop now, and knew he should go and find the boys and tell them about keeping a watch for strangers. Instead, he urged the horses to carry on one more time. Approaching the steel hoop Daniel prepared for a move he'd only recently started practising and launched himself off Savage's back – legs straight, toes pointed, arms held close, body twisting left shoulder over right in the air in a graceful spiral flip.

As he turned he could hear Billy yell his name, but there was no stopping now. He'd realized a long time ago that actually doing a trick was never the problem, it was the thinking about doing it that made you nervous; so now he just went ahead and did it. Then he was spreading out his arms and legs, almost floating down so that, as he fell between the horses – any audience sure he was going to land in between their stamping hooves on the ground – his hands grabbed their manes and his feet hooked over near their rumps. With one last push Daniel sprang upwards and there he was, sitting on Snowdrop's back. He pulled her mane back to slow her down, Savage sensing the move and slowing too.

*Daniel prepared for a move he'd only recently started practising.*

"One day, Danny-boy, one day..."

"One day what, Billy?"

"You'll be the death of me, that's what, pulling stunts when I ain't expecting it – you going to do that again tonight?"

"Thinking I might."

"You doing it to impress Mr. Hubble's lady friend?"

Daniel jumped off Snowdrop. "No, no I ain't."

"Fine, because I want you keeping your mind on what you're doing, and not wondering what people are thinking of you or who's watching. Else you'll end up in the sawdust and they'll think you're a fool."

## CHAPTER 5

# LADIES AND GENTLEMEN!

"What's she like, Danny?" Seth was walking backwards as he talked, his hands a blur as he juggled two apples and a pear. With half an hour or so before the first performance, the three friends were wandering round the outskirts of the campsite, Daniel already with his hair greased and pulled back and wearing his black woollen tights with the gold stripe sewn down the side.

"Josie?"

"Oooh!" Seth rolled his eyes. "It's Josie now, is it!"

Daniel ignored him. "She's very nice, far as I could tell...wasn't there for long."

"Me dad said she had a fine figure, an' me mam hit him with a pan." Jem sniggered at the memory as he took a bite out of his apple.

"What kind of strangers did Mr. Hubble say we was s'posed to be looking for?" Unexpectedly Seth threw a flying apple at Daniel, who grabbed it out of the air, grinning. The other two pieces of fruit dropped into Seth's hands and he began eating the pear. "'Cos this place is full of 'em every night."

"He didn't say exactly...anyone acting suspicious, I s'pose, just keep an eye out. Keep 'em peeled is what he said, Seth."

"Wonder why she came here."

"Her father was a good friend of his, like I told you...they used to be in the ring, bare-knuckle fighters." Much as he wanted to show off that he'd got other information, Daniel left things at that, knowing he'd be for it if he said any more.

"What do we do if we spot anything?"

"Ask 'em ever so nice if they'd mind goin' away, Jem!" Seth lobbed his half-eaten pear at him. "We go an' get help, you dullard – right, Daniel?"

"Best do that."

"We've not had any trouble for some time, life's been reasonable to us these last few months." Seth, who tumbled and juggled on the show-front to entertain those turning up for the performances, began walking on his hands as easily as he did on his feet. "Can't fathom why they don't like us anyway...what did we ever do but make 'em laugh?"

"Reckon they're jealous." Daniel finished off his apple and threw the core over to where a couple of dogs lay resting under a caravan. "Being stuck in one place all their lives."

"I wouldn't mind being stuck in the same place for a week or so, specially when it rains an' we got to push wagons out of the mud," grinned Jem.

"Come on..." With no warning Daniel started running. "I've got to get into the rest of my costume – race you back to mine!"

They'd managed to get three shorter thruppenny performances in before the sun began to set and the naphtha lamps had to be lit. There'd already been one good sixpenny show this Saturday night and as Daniel paraded Savage and Snowdrop across the show-front – Mr. Hubble, in tails and with his best top hat on the side of his head, ringing a handbell and doing his patter – he could see they'd have a good crowd for the last show as well. Marlborough was going to do them proud, everyone's pockets were going to be full and, even though five performances was a lot of work, they all knew, the next day being Sunday, they'd have it a little easier with a later start and no ring work till Monday.

Leading the horses off the show-front and into the tent, Daniel took them back across the ring and behind the red curtain to where they'd wait for their turn in front of the audience. As he tied them up he saw Comus; maybe now was the moment they could have a talk.

In his white clown costume, whited-up face, exaggerated mouth and eyes and red nose the old clown looked odd, like a cross between a young man and an old man. Patting Savage, Daniel went over to where Comus was relaxing, sitting on a bale of straw and smoking a pipe, and sat next to him.

Behind them the bell rang, a trumpet blared and cymbals crashed as Mr. Hubble, who, once he put his showman's costume on, became a different person, gave the crowd a description of what delights awaited them tonight inside the tent.

"...and we have got for you a pair of dancing dogs, the like of which you will have never seen!" he bellowed. "Believe me, because I would not lie to you good people – and we have *The Professorial Donkey*... I see from the look on yer face, sir, that you are thinking, 'How can that possibly be? A donkey is in the way of being quite the most stupid of animals!' Well, sir, *this* donkey, while it would not, I admit, get into the likes of Oxford University, is a most *excellent* mathematician..."

Comus tamped his pipe down with a tar-brown finger. "Sorry I've not had a chance to talk to you since yesterday, Danny-boy."

"That's all right."

"Bruise tells me you met Josie." Daniel nodded. "Lucky for the girl she takes after her mother, as I did hear Morgan Finnister wasn't the prettiest of sights even before he started fighting."

"Mr. Hubble told me there were people looking for her, which was why she's come down here."

"He did, did he? Did he also tell you you could talk about it?"

Daniel's mouth went dry. "I thought you'd...I thought he...Mr. Hubble, I thought he'd've told you..."

"Happen he did, Daniel, but don't never take for granted what you don't know for a fact. And that, I can tell you, is advice I learned the hard way."

"I've not told anyone, like Mr. Hubble said; the others just think they're looking out for hooligans, nothing more, Comus, I promise." Comus puffed on his clay pipe and nodded. "What's she taken, Comus...why did she steal something?"

"What did I tell you before, boy?"

Daniel got up and kicked at the straw littering the ground. "You wouldn't tell me, even if you could, as it's not any of my business."

"That's the way it is."

"But—"

"No buts about it, young Daniel!"

"I'm not sayin' there are...it's about what I told you the other evening...about seeing those things, Comus. If I saw her, I mean Josie, if I saw her like she really is – and I did, Comus, you know I did – what of the fire I saw, does that mean it's really going to happen too?"

"Come back and sit here." Comus patted the space next to him on the bale. "And don't be frightened."

"I keep on thinking what Hannah would say...that it's the likes of witchcraft." Daniel sat down, leaning forward, elbows on his knees, head in his hands. "I don't want to be a charmer, I don't want people looking at me like I was...like I was somebody bad. I just want to ride Savage, that's all, Comus."

"I know, and I can't promise anything I say is going to make you feel any the better about it, Danny-boy. Except that, in my mind, it's got nothing to do with evil or the Devil or any of that harum-scarum nonsense."

"Hannah doesn't think it's nonsense, she never liked it when I used to tell her about my dreams. She'd always cross herself an' whisper prayers about it."

"And Billy?"

"Billy's never said."

"You ever asked him?"

"No."

"Why not?"

"Whatever he thinks, he keeps it to himself, Comus, specially if it's different from what Hannah thinks."

A chuckle like a throaty purr rose in Comus's throat. "Such wisdom in one so young!"

"What am I to do, though?"

"I been thinking, since we last talked." Comus chewed on his pipe stem. "And it occurs to me that the best protection is prevention, wouldn't you say?"

"How can I stop seeing these things – they just happen to me!"

"I don't mean that, boy...not much as we can do about that at the moment but not worry. What I *meant* was the fire."

"But how do we stop the fire occurring if I've seen it happen?"

"Keep a watch, Danny-boy – keep a watch! Which you already have the lads doing, ain't that right?" Daniel nodded. "Well then, as you've some time on yer hands till the next show, don't sit on yer thumbs and idle about – go and see they're doing their job!"

Outside the tent the night smelled of excitement. It had been like this Daniel's whole life, but he still felt the tingle, the shiver down his back as events moved forward to the start of a final show of the night, like music to a crescendo. Whatever it was, this feeling of anticipation, it was in the air and he realized it was partly brought in by the people coming to see the performance, and partly it came from the circus folk themselves, knowing they had to come up to expectations.

All around him was bustle and shouting and laughter and people moving in every direction. Here, where the sideshows and peep shows and attractions were, was not where eyes should be kept peeled. This was not where Daniel had seen the fire. That was back behind the big tent, where the wagons and caravans were, where strangers shouldn't be. Slipping into the shadows, Daniel went in search of Jem, Seth and the other boys he'd given the instructions to keep their eyes peeled.

Over the years the motley band of children had developed a way of communicating between themselves, inventing a system using bird calls. As he walked, Daniel cupped his hands and made the chattering sound of a magpie, almost instantly getting a reply from way over to his right and another not very far away to his left; his eyes now pretty well adjusted to the dark, he made his way towards the nearest person, somewhere up ahead in the gloom.

"Danny?"

Daniel stopped as a slight figure wrapped in a shawl stepped out, silhouetted against a lighter wedge of sky between two wagons; he recognized Jem's younger sister. "Flo? You in on this?"

"More eyes the better, right? I ain't seen nothing, though."

"Where's Jem?"

"He said he was going to walk all around, like in a big circle...left a bit ago, shouldn't be long, I expect."

A shrill peewit call came from behind him and Daniel turned to see Jem trotting his way. "Seen anything?"

"Nothing ain't s'posed to be there, Danny, none of us have."

"No one wandering round?" Jem shook his head. "Best keep going till the show's over, then we'll see what Mr. Hubble says to do."

"They all seem very friendly, these people here." Jem dug something out of his waistcoat pocket, bent slightly and struck a lucifer on his lifted boot heel, a ball of fire spitting furiously into life at the end of the wooden stick he held between his fingers; the air was filled with light and the sharp whiff of sulphur. "Know what? I don't reckon there's going to be trouble here tonight." He grinned, shadows dancing on his up-lit face, making him look like a leering devil, and flicked the match into the air.

Daniel watched the flame arc towards the ground, stunned at what he was seeing, the thought exploding into his head – could this be how the fire started? He leaped forward. "No, Jem!"

"What?"

Daniel stamped on the dying match as it hit the ground. "Could start a fire!"

"It went out...wasn't going to start no fire, Danny – was it, Flo?"

Flo sucked in her bottom lip, wondering what had made Daniel overreact so. "Didn't look like it."

"I'd better get back to the tent..." Daniel glanced from Jem to Flo, both looking at him, puzzled; they didn't know what he'd seen; they had no idea how panicked the simple act of striking a match had made him, and there was no way he could explain it to them. "Else I'll be late..."

# CHAPTER 6
# THE WATCHERS

Hampton Dooley took a nip of Jamaican rum and screwed the cap back on his hip flask; he felt its harsh warmth spreading down his throat to his stomach, and thought, as he often did when taking a tipple, that this was as near as he was ever going to get to the Indies. "What's the plan then, Jake?"

"For you not to get so boozy you can't stand up straight, Aitch." Jacob Husker reached over and swiped the metal flask out of Dooley's hand and shook it to see how much rum was left. "And for us to get this blistering job over an' done with so we can get back to London... What's she doing out here in the sticks anyway? Why's she hanging round with a travelling show?"

"Getting as far away from Mr. Bland as she can?" Dooley snapped his fingers. "Give us back me rum, Jake, it's just to keep me warm."

"It's a summer's night, Aitch, and you ain't cold – and if she'd wanted to get away she should've got on a boat and done the job proper." Husker slipped the flask into his coat pocket. "Are you sure the lad at the inn said she come out here?"

Dooley nodded. "He said she hired a pony an' trap when she got off the train, an' said this is where she asked the bloke to take her. How long are we going to have to wait here, Jake? There's all kinds of animals in the country come out at night..."

"There's a lot more much bigger animals in that circus, and people, what come out at night; all we have to do is wait till they all go to their beds and then get on with what we've come to do."

"How're we going to know where she is?"

"That has been exercising me somewhat, Aitch, I'll admit it has." Husker pulled open a brass spyglass and peered through it. "It's too dark for this to be much use, so, we'll have to go an' take a look around."

"What if we don't get her tonight?"

"An easy job'll turn into a harder one, Aitch." Husker snapped the spyglass shut and put it away inside his coat. "Mr. Bland wants Josie Finnister back in town, and be quick about it. He does not want us swanning round the countryside following a gaggle of freaks, tumblers and showmen. So we've got to get the job over and done with, Aitch. No two ways about it. We only get paid when the job's done and dusted, remember, which in this case is the kidnapping and safe delivery of Miss Finnister."

"Two hunner'd fifty guineas is a lot of gilt for a skirt what looks after an alehouse and run off with the takings, Jake, wouldn't you say?"

"I would, Aitch, I would." Husker cleared his throat and spat. "Which means, more'n likely, she ain't just a skirt what runs an alehouse. But that's not fer us to know, is it? Otherwise Mr. Bland would've said... Right, let's go an' take a look at this ragtag mob, see where she is..."

Jacob Husker was a thin, wiry man, not so tall and with a slight limp – the result of breaking his ankle when he was a strip of a boy, jumping from a first storey window of a house he'd been caught attempting to burgle. Jacob had been lucky in more ways than one that night: he hadn't been caught, which would otherwise have meant the gallows, and his break hadn't gone bad on him, so he'd kept his foot attached to his leg.

He'd worked for Carter Bland, more on than off, for some few years now. A ragged orphan, he'd made his way up from the dirt-poor streets of St Giles by stealing and dodging and fighting his way out into a life of fresher air, better clothes and food when he was hungry. All the things that money could buy and staying in the slums would never get you. Jacob Husker would happily lie to St Peter at the Pearly Gates, but he'd promised himself he'd never, ever go back to living like he had as a child, that he'd die in his boots before he did.

Jacob knew Carter Bland used him because he had a reputation for being clever and ruthless – but mainly because he was guaranteed to be as loyal as a dog for as long as you paid him well, which made him almost trustworthy. Jacob used Hampton Dooley, on the other hand, because he was as strong as a bulldog and not quite as bright. Aitch wasn't going to see much, if any, of his share of the fee for this job, as Jacob had plans. He was going to do what Josie Finnister should've done: get on a boat and go to America, see what New York could do for a man who'd done well enough for himself in London.

And he had done well. Not as well as Carter Bland, it was true, but then Carter Bland had been born lucky. Carter's father, Elliot Bland, had been a merchant, and a very successful one; spices, sugar, tobacco and more came into the warehouses of E. Bland & Sons down in the East End, and cloth, crockery and such went out the other way. Elliot Bland supplied what people demanded.

Quite why Carter hadn't been satisfied with living off the fat of his father's land, Jacob didn't know. It must, he thought, be something to do with being the youngest of old Mr. Bland's three surviving sons. With their father dead, the oldest brother now ran the importing side of the business, the other one handling exports to the Empire, and it had at first occurred to Jacob that maybe Carter was bored as there was no real place for him in the business. But then he'd quickly discovered the simple truth: Carter was just a bad, rich boy with a decidedly evil streak. And Jacob knew a stinker when he saw one.

Carter had started his own business, out of his father's sight and away from his brothers' prying eyes, but with the indulgent acceptance of his gorgon of a mother. While her hair wasn't made of live snakes and Jacob had never witnessed her turning anyone into stone, he'd seen enough to know that Renée Bland wasn't someone to be trifled with, and that Carter definitely took after his mother. To those who worked for the family she was known – out of earshot, naturally – as The Queen, or more often Queenie, and in her eyes her youngest and most favoured son could do no wrong. Evil mother begets a wicked son; two dark creatures you'd never want to turn your back on.

In a house to the north of Soho Square, Carter Bland ran a gaming establishment he called The Ace of Clubs, an establishment specializing in carefully loaded dice, artfully marked cards and any number of ways to make its own luck. Jacob never went to The Ace to play, believing that betting was enough of a mug's game to start with without also removing the element of chance. He only walked through the doors when called in to be given his tasks – Carter often needed debts collected or information acquired about his clientele.

This latest job had seemed simple enough: find out where a slip called Josie Finnister, who ran an inn Carter Bland owned down near Clerkenwell, had gone. She looked after some place called The Sun, which Jacob, so far as he remembered, had never been to as he preferred to stay up West. All Jacob had to do, Carter had said, was nab the girl and bring her and whatever she had with her back to The Ace; Carter had been uncharacteristically vague about why he wanted the girl, giving the impression Josie'd gone with the week's proceeds, nothing more than that.

Jacob, who had always found it a good idea never to believe everything he was told, did some digging and poking around of his own; in his experience, the truth was more likely to be found swept under a carpet than in plain view out in the sunlight. Much more likely. It turned out, once Jacob had greased a few palms, that Josie, the little vixen, had stolen something – papers, someone thought it might be, jewellery was another opinion – from The Ace and Carter Bland wanted it back bad enough to pay handsomely.

So far, so nice and simple.

The only real problem was that Hampton Dooley had been with Jacob when exactly how much Mr. Bland was prepared to pay had been mentioned, and it was clear he now thought he was in for his fair share. Still, Jacob thought as he watched Aitch's shadowy figure in front of him as they made their way towards the circus, this life was full of disappointments. He usually worked alone, but this job required the lifting of a live one and an extra pair of hands was essential – though as soon as the girl was delivered to the back entrance of The Ace, Jacob would return to working solo. In fact, he'd be buying himself a one-way passage across the Atlantic and Aitch could whistle for his money.

Finding out where Josie had gone hadn't been easy, but then, as Jacob always said, if the jobs Carter Bland used him for were easy, anyone could do them. In the process of learning where Josie had gone, Jacob dredged up a few other pearls of information, such as that The Sun, the inn she was managing for young Mr. Bland, used to belong to her father and, so the story went, it had been "won" by Carter in a fixed game of cards. More fool Morgan Finnister, Jacob had thought when he'd heard the tale, for not being more careful whom he played cards with.

Morgan Finnister had died not long afterwards, one of Jacob's informants had told him. An ill-considered last fight, for a purse that he apparently wanted to use to try and buy The Sun back from Bland, had done for him; he'd been beaten to a bloody pulp by a younger, fitter man he never should've fought and twelve-year-old Josie had been left to fend for herself and her grieving mother.

Jacob was rarely touched by other people's calamities, as, in his opinion, the sods usually brought their bad fortune on themselves, and even though Josie's mother had also died not long after her husband, at least Josie hadn't been thrown out onto the filthy streets of Babylon. At least she hadn't had to bear the indignity and inhumanity of that life. Instead, she'd been taken into the Bland household, given a roof and a job – even if it was skivvy work. Then, and Jacob did think this showed the cruel side of Carter Bland's nature, when she was older she'd been made to go and look after the alehouse that had been her father's and where she'd grown up.

If she'd stolen from the man paying his wages, Jacob could quite understand why. In fact, he thought Bland lucky that that was all she'd tried to do. Revenge, in his world, usually took a more permanent form. Life was cheap and vengeance and retribution, no matter what the priests might tell you, weren't only the Lord's for the taking. If he'd been in Josie's place Carter Bland would have died a long, slow and painful death. Very painful...

"...Jake?"

"What?" Jacob Husker's mind snapped from imagining how he'd kill Carter Bland, if he should ever need to, back to the present.

"I said, what now, Jake? We're there."

Husker walked up next to Dooley and stopped. Ahead, just past some scrub bushes, were the outskirts of the circus, pale, flickering globes of light from oil lamps picking out parts of tents and caravans and wagons.

"We'll go round the front, Aitch." Jacob nodded to himself. "Like we was anyone else, coming to see the show. Then we look out for Miss Finnister." Husker reached into his coat.

"You giving me back me rum, Jake?"

"You'll get that when we've done our work and not before... I'm getting out the sketch Mr. Bland give me." From his coat Husker pulled a folded piece of paper and opened it up, holding it so he could better see the pen drawing of a young woman's face. "He says this is a good likeness and all we have to keep in mind is that she has red hair, copper-red hair. Shouldn't be hard to spot..."

# CHAPTER 7
# On the Lookout

The band was in full flight, two trumpets and a squeeze box accompanied by a large, perspiring youth on drums, cymbals and tambourine; all the instruments were being played with more enthusiasm and brio than musical expertise as half a dozen clowns, under Comus's direction, mugged it up for the audience.

Daniel had seen this sort of act all his life and now, more than what was going on in the ring, he loved to sit, hidden in the shadows, and watch the faces of the audience as the clowns did their business. The children, especially, were the ones he loved the most; small faces full of wonder, eyes wide with amazement. They'd be laughing one moment and shocked the next when they thought someone actually had hurt themselves, that a pretend kick to the backside – together with a hefty thump on the big drum and bang of cymbals – was real.

Then Mr. Hubble appeared and with a crack of his whip he sent the clowns scurrying in all directions as he bellowed, "And now, for your delectation, amusement and ultimate *amazement*, I should like to introduce to you: *Baron Magnus, the Mighty Ox*!"

As the band's music rose to a crescendo of crashing cymbals and trumpet flourishes the curtain was flung aside and Sam Baston, stripped to the waist and dressed in white trousers with a blood-red silk sash as a belt, strode into the ring, stopping every few steps to strike a pose that would show off his magnificently sculpted muscles. He looked like an ebony statue somehow brought magically to life.

Behind him came two horses pulling a low cart with Sam's weights on it, the message for the audience being – look, it takes TWO HORSES to pull what Baron Magnus is going to lift up! Then a couple of burly riggers made a big drama of taking the weights off the cart, grimacing and straining and staggering from the effort. Sam never spoke during his act, letting Mr. Hubble talk the audience through what he was doing.

"Ladeeez and gent-el-men!" he'd say after Sam had dropped the largest weights after lifting them, a look of complete and utter astonishment on his face. "Ladeeez and gent-el-*men* – did you feel that? It was as if the very *earth* itself moved!"

Sam's finale was to stand, legs planted firmly apart, hands on hips, as the tumblers, using a springboard, built a towering pyramid of six people on his broad shoulders. Once that was complete and the crowd thought they'd seen everything, Mr. Hubble would search the audience for two lady volunteers, asking them to sit in canvas seats Sam was holding in each hand, which he would then proceed to lift up off the ground to rousing cheers. As the ladies went back to their seats, the tumblers dropped to the ground like autumn leaves and ran to the curtain, leaving Sam to take his bow and collect his well-deserved applause.

There were now only a couple of acts left before it was Daniel's turn, so he left his vantage point and went back to put his jacket on and make sure everything was fine with the horses.

* * *

Jacob Husker watched his companion, who was completely transfixed by the performance, laughing at the childish antics of the clowns, slapping his thighs and cheering as the impressive Baron Magnus, silent as a carving, picked up weights as if they were mere feather pillows.

As far as he could tell, the Finnister girl wasn't in the crowd and now, while the show was in full swing, might be a good time to have a look outside. He leaned across and tapped Dooley on the shoulder.

"Aitch?"

Dooley glanced to his right, smiling at his companion. "That Baron, he's a sight, wouldn't you say, Jake?"

"Granted, Aitch, but not the one what we've come here to see." Husker stood up.

"Where you goin', Jake?"

Husker bent down, whispering in Dooley's ear. "You stay here, keep an eye out fer Josie – you never know, she might even be part of an act – and I'll take a look outside." He stood up, then ducked down again. "I'll either come back in, or meet you outside after, all right?"

Dooley, his attention drawn back to the ring, nodded and stuck his thumb up. Shaking his head, Husker made his way along the row they were sitting in, jumped awkwardly down to ground level and made his way outside the tent.

Keeping to the shadows, he walked quietly away from the big top, in the direction he'd seen earlier would take him to where the caravans and tents had been pitched for the night. Stopping for a moment, he got Dooley's hip flask out of his coat, uncapped it and took a slug, wiping his lips on the back of his sleeve. Husker's eyes were by now used to the dark: he could see as good as he was ever going to in what moonlight there was and so he set off again; he'd only gone a few yards when his feet seemed to tangle with something and he tripped, landing on his face in the damp grass.

A young voice, a girl's, came from behind him. "Where you going, mister?"

Husker rolled sideways, sat up and looked round, frowning. "Who's that, wanting to know?"

"You got no business round here, mister."

"'Pologies, miss." Husker reached for his hat, stood up and wiped his hands on his trousers, wondering who this gobby little mite thought she was. He bent down and brushed his knees, glad he'd thought to wear his old green suit on this job and not one of his newer ones. "I need a piss, I was looking fer the jakes."

"They ain't round here. Go back the way you come."

Husker looked down at the girl, all of eight, nine years of her, looking sternly back up at him, holding the stick she must've tripped him with. He could walk straight past her, easy, push her out of the way, no trouble. But that was the point, he didn't want any trouble and he was sure that's what she'd make if he didn't do what she said.

"Back that way?" Husker pointed behind him, wobbling slightly like he might've had a little too much to drink and then standing ramrod straight. "That's where I'll go then." The girl just nodded.

As Husker carefully put his hat back on, the door of a small wagon a few yards away opened, lamplight spilling out into the night, followed by the silhouetted figure of a woman, her red hair almost glowing like polished copper. Husker caught her profile as she turned to put out the lamp and close the door, above which, he noticed, the word "Rosalie" was painted. Josie Finnister. No doubt about it.

He turned and without another word made his way past the girl and back towards the big top, walking in a way he hoped made it look like he was tipsy. He was smiling, not that there was anyone to notice, and in his mind Jacob Husker was walking with a strut and clicking his heels.

*Josie Finnister. No doubt about it.*

* * *

"Jem!"

"Not now, Flo...got to go an' help clear the ring for Daniel." Jem was about to run off when he saw his sister's face and stopped. "What is it, Flo?"

"I saw someone."

"You saw someone?"

Flo nodded. "Like Daniel said, someone what shouldn't be where they were."

"Look, I'll get skinned if I don't go." Jem glanced round. "See Comus over there? You tell him, an' I'll be back as soon as I've finished."

Watching her brother sprint away and disappear through the curtains, Flo went over and sat down next to the old clown. "Comus?"

"Child?"

"You know about us having to keep a watch, case someone tries something? Like what happened before." Comus nodded. "Well I saw someone. A man. Said he was looking for the jakes, but he wasn't; tried to make it look like he'd had a few drinks, too, but he hadn't."

"How d'you know so much?"

"You can tell, Comus."

"Well, that's true enough." Comus frowned. "What did you do?"

"I was hid, an' I saw him, skulking, an' I tripped

him." Flo held up her stick. "Then I asked him what he was doing where he shouldn't be."

"You did? Truly?" Flo nodded. "And what did this person do then?"

"Like I said, he made out like he needed the jakes an' that he was tipsy, which he weren't. I watched him come my way an' he was walking normal, 'ceptin' he had a limp a bit like what Billy has; an' I saw him take a drink, so's he'd smell like he had, I reckon."

"Where was this?"

"Over by the caravan where that new lady is."

"The new lady."

"She came out, I saw her."

"Did the man see her?"

"Prob'ly."

"Did he say anything when he did?"

Flo shook her head. "Just walked back the way he'd come."

"Wonder where he went...?"

"Back in the tent, I followed for a bit."

"Regular little detective, you are!"

"Did I do good?"

"Better'n good, child." Comus got up and stretched. "Not long till the show's over...let's us go round the front, find somewhere to put ourselves so's we can see the folk come out the tent. See if you can spot your man again."

* * *

Hampton Dooley was engrossed in a display of horse-riding skills – a young boy leaping though rings of fire – as Jacob Husker slipped back into the space on the bench next to him, nudging him as he did so. "I've seen her."

Dooley hardly glanced at him. "Who?"

"Josie, who else?"

"You been at me rum, Jake – give it me back!"

"That all in the world you care about? Come on, we're going…" Husker stood up.

"But the show's not finished!"

"You will be, if you don't shift yer pudden arse!" Husker pushed his way back along the bench, ignoring the looks he was getting from the people he was having to step over for the third time. Jumping back down onto the ground, careful not to land on his bad ankle, he waited for Dooley to join him.

"I was enjoying that." Dooley looked like a child who'd had some sweet titbit taken away from it. "They had a edjacated donkey."

"Maybe I should get him to help me next time."

"Where we going?"

"Find ourselves a tavern, rest up fer a bit."

"Then what?"

"Then, Aitch, when it's well past the witching hour,

we'll quietly make our return and finish the job off…get ourselves on the road back to the Smoke."

Outside the big tent, sitting on the steps of a darkened caravan, Comus lit his pipe again, the lucifer flaring as he flicked it with his thumbnail. "Can you see all right, Flo?"

"Just perfeck, Comus."

"You stay back there in the shadows, so's your man don't see you're observing him."

There had been a steady trickle of people going in and out of the tent, always was, even coming up to the end of a performance; calls of nature to be answered, arguments to be settled, all kinds of reasons why folk couldn't sit still and watch, thought Comus, puffing on his lit pipe. Still, long as they'd paid their money he supposed it was up to them whether they watched or not. Then he saw two men come out, one smaller than the other and with a limp, as Flo had said, a lot like Billy's.

"Comus!" hissed an excited voice behind him.

"Quiet, child... I seen 'em." Comus watched as the pair walked off, the bigger of the two hanging back and looking over his shoulder as if he'd left someone behind; he saw the smaller man stop and tell his friend to get a move on.

"Should we follow 'em?"

Comus watched as the two men walked away in the opposite direction to Josie's caravan. "They're leaving, Flo...best we can do is find Bruise and tell him what you seen." From inside the tent came a big cheer and the crash of cymbals. "Sounds like Daniel's doing well tonight – shall we go and catch the end?"

Flo came out of the shadows behind him and stood on the top step. "D'you think they'll be back?"

"Need a crystal ball to know that, child..."

# CHAPTER 8
# FINALE!

Josie Finnister stood at the side of the curtain watching Daniel's performance, spellbound at the sight of this boy who seemed to be able to dance in the air, leaping, almost flying from one horse to the other. And now he was jumping through steel rings of fire as if fire was his friend and would do no more than stroke him gently. He surely was a talent, just like Bruise had told her.

She glanced at the crowd, catching people as

wide-eyed at what they were watching as she was, all of them clapping as Daniel spun back upright and landed, one foot on the black horse the other on the white. He'd been in the ring for quite a few minutes and Josie half expected that last trick to be the end of his part of the show, but instead of finishing it looked like he was geeing the horses on rather than slowing them down.

Round the circle the black and the white horses thundered, only inches between them, Daniel rock solid on their backs; at the last possible moment the boy – his long, shiny black hair tied in a ponytail flying behind him – launched himself through the still-flaming ring just like he had before. But this time, after he twisted in mid-air, he didn't land on his feet but seemed to be diving for the ground! Almost as one the crowd gasped, thinking, like Josie, that Daniel must be going to fall between the horses and hit the sawdust – how could he be making such a terrible mistake?

But he wasn't.

At the very last moment Daniel's arms and legs suddenly shot out sideways, his feet catching the rear of the horses, his hands their manes; bending like a bow, Daniel somehow powered himself back up and then there he was, sitting astride the black horse, a huge smile on his face, bowing and waving to the ecstatic crowd as if he really was Crown Prince Juan

Pablo of Nicobar. This time the crowd stood and roared their appreciation, stamping their feet and clapping as Daniel cantered out of the ring and Mr. Hubble strode back in, cracking his whip like a pistol shot.

"Have you *ever* seen the like of it before?" Josie heard him bellow as she ducked through a gap in the rough canvas and went looking for Daniel to tell him what an amazing show he'd put on. "Did I not *say* to you good people that seeing was believing? Before your very eyes, ladeez and gent-el-men – as promised to you by my good self – feats of the most elegant, most exciting and most *extraordinary* equestrian prowess!"

Behind her Josie could hear the band strike up a new tune and around her order was appearing out of chaos as all the performers readied themselves to parade through the curtains one last time and take their bow. At the end of the snaking line of costumed acrobats, jugglers and clowns, whose make-up was beginning to look in need of repair, she saw Daniel rubbing down the white horse and went over to him.

"Daniel?" The boy looked round. "You must've heard this a thousand times, and that crowd, well, you know they loved you...but I just wanted to say I thought you were a marvel to watch, just as good as Bruise made you out to be. He must be very proud of you."

"Thank you...very kind, ma'am..."

"Josie, call me Josie, like I said."

Out in the ring there was a mighty crashing of cymbals and it sounded like the trumpeters were killing cats instead of playing music; then the curtains were drawn back and the line of performers began to march out into the ring. Daniel leaped up onto the back of the black horse, leaning forward to stroke his smooth, lustrous neck.

"Pardon me, ma'am...Josie...but I got to go."

Something about the way the boy acted made Josie think he was nervous around her, though why that should be she couldn't imagine, them having only just met. Maybe, during the time she was going to spend with the circus, he'd get to know her a bit better.

There turned out to be an inn, not far from where the circus was pitched, that was still open when Dooley took the brougham into its yard. The landlord was happy enough to take Husker's money for his ostler to be woken and got up out of his pit to look after the horse.

If there were guineas on the bar some food and drink could also be provided, of course it could, and the two gentlemen from London wanted a room prepared for them, even if they only wanted to use it for a few hours? Why, walk this way, good sirs! Generally, when a man with what appeared to be deep pockets asked a question, Husker had found the answer was likely to be yes.

The beef hotpot was, as promised, hot, and the beef more than palatable; the beer was better than a lot of the muck they served up in certain taverns in London and the bed comfortable, if small. Husker made Dooley take the chair on the principle that he was the one needed his wits about him, while all Dooley had to do was do as he was told.

"How're we going to know when to wake?"

"We ain't going to sleep, Aitch."

"Ain't going...what've we taken a room for then?"

"Because I for one'd rather be under a roof while I was waiting, and not lodged in a carriage, listening to the horse fart. Also, I had a pocket of Carter Bland's money I didn't see much point in giving back to him."

"I wonder what it's like being so rich you don't care too much about yer money, just hand it out like it was monkey nuts."

Husker undid the laces on one of his boots and pulled it off, revealing a dark-brown sock with a hole through which his big toe was poking; he looked over at Dooley, pondering that he'd soon have more than enough money to buy a whole new wardrobe of clothes. "You think Mr. Bland don't care about his money you'd be very wrong...the reason he ain't married is he's already in love with his lucre."

"S'pose that's why we're out here, getting that thieving little article Josie Finnister back, right?"

"Very perspicacious of you, Aitch...very likely that's the case."

The two men fell silent for a few minutes, Husker taking off his other boot and Dooley reaching over and lighting a new candle from the guttering remains in the candlestick.

"Jake?"

"Aitch."

"What if we fall asleep?"

"The moment you begin to snore, I'll throw this boot at you..."

As the last of the audience wended its way out of the tent and into the night, happy that they'd invested their hard-earned pennies wisely in a remarkable evening's entertainment, Comus walked over to where Mr. Hubble was standing. The small girl accompanying him clung like a shadow, trying to keep out of eyeshot. She'd never actually spoken to the big man before.

"Bruise, got a moment?"

Hubble looked at his friend, spotting that he'd got someone with him. "What is it?"

Comus shepherded his small companion round to his side. “Flo here, well, she was helping the lads keep a watch on the environs, like you asked Daniel to get sorted.”

Hubble looked down at the little girl. “You Jem’s sister?” Flo nodded and Hubble glanced at Comus. “Something not right?”

“Flo saw something, Bruise, a man wandering round the back,” he paused, “close by where Josie’s caravan is.” Comus saw the big bear of a man stop and frown, suddenly taking everything being said more seriously.

Hubble peered down at the small child. “What was he doing there?”

Flo remained silent, staring back at him.

“Ain’t going to bite, Flo...” Comus patted her shoulder.

“He was pretending, Mr. Hubble, sir.”

“Pretending, child? Pretending what?”

Comus felt Flo grip his hand as Hubble raised his voice. “She says he was making out to be a bit tipsy, Bruise, and like he was looking for the jakes. But he wasn’t, Flo here saw him acting quite normal, then take a drink so’s he’d smell right. He was with another man, they’d been watching the show...we saw them come out.”

“Where’d they go?”

"Away, off the site, Bruise."

"Did you follow 'em?"

Comus shook his head. "Couldn't send a child on a job like that, and I'd be no good..."

"Right...a'course...we'll just have to keep a watch on all night, Comus...best we can do." Hubble frowned, rubbing his scarred face thoughtfully. "I got more than enough to occupy meself with right now – can you look after this? And make sure those you pick know what these flash-coves look like."

Hubble turned to walk away and then stopped, bending down till he was looking Flo straight in her small, pale face. "Near forgot me manners, child... here's two penn'orth for yer good work."

Comus watched Hubble's great, broad back disappear through the curtains, thinking how few people ever saw the soft side of the man; it was either the gruff boss or the loud showman, rarely anything in between. He looked down at Flo, standing next to him examining the coins in her hand. "Two penn'orth, eh, Flo? Fair pay, I'd say, but we got a little more work to do. Come on..."

There'd be no one in the circus who wasn't tired after the hard day they'd had, working from before dawn till long after dusk. Thinking things over in his mind,

Comus reckoned if he had two people walking round the site, all cudgelled up, and changed them every hour or so, that should do the job. And he'd use the older boys with no families that needed looking to and who'd have the energy for a bit of extra work, especially if they thought the circus might be expecting any kind of trouble.

As he and Flo walked out of the big tent, Comus saw Seth with a couple more young riggers and called them over. A quarter of an hour or so later, outside his caravan Comus was holding court, Flo sitting behind him on the top step, and a dozen pairs of youthful eyes and ears were pinned back and eager to hear what he had on his mind.

"Let's say, for the sake of an argument, it takes about ten minutes to walk slowly round the perimeter of the site, one person going clockwise, the other in the opposite direction...yes?" Comus watched the heads in front of him nod in agreement. "So I say, after six, mebbe seven times of going round, those two then waking the next two up, an' so on until dawn, should do the trick of keeping us safe. And you all know that there are two coves we're after in partic'ler, the one Flo here saw, wearing a greenish suit, not too tall, with a limp, and his bigger mate. You see 'em, you beat the merry Hell out of them!"

That brought a ragged cheer from the assembled company, most of whom had been around the last time the circus had had trouble and relished the chance to crack the skulls of anyone trying it on again. As Comus waved goodbye to the group, taking Flo off to her family's caravan, a wild screeching cut through the night air.

"It's that Tom feller," Seth grinned. "The one that sounds like he plays the trumpet with his arse.

"Bet you that's those two little tearaways, Mickey 'n' Ron," another voice called out. "Bet they've found a local cat an' chucked it in with some of the dogs again!"

"You find 'em, Sy, you tell 'em from me to get to their beds, or else!" Comus shook his head. "This ain't the time for silly games."

# CHAPTER 9
# RED SKY AT NIGHT

If Sy Tennant had been able to put money on his bet that Ron and Mickey were behind the disturbance, he would've won. It was a game they'd had their ears boxed before for playing, but one they never tired of, only this time it didn't play out the way they thought it would. Normally, whatever poor cat they caught and threw in where the dogs were sleeping got chased for as long as it took for the creature to find its way up out of reach; where it would have to stay until the mutts got bored with waiting for it to come down and went away.

This time was different.

The boys knew they had a fighter from the scratches they'd both received getting it into the sack in the first place. The cat, a lean, sprightly ginger tom with a surprisingly vicious temper, then flew into a rage the moment they tipped it out of the sack and it hit the ground; spitting and yowling, its fur fluffed out so it looked twice the size, its razor-sharp claws scythed anything within range. Momentarily taken aback by the ferocity of this orange fury that had been dropped unannounced into their midst, the dogs, half a dozen of them, circled the cat and then attacked. And so did the cat.

Hacking its way up the nearest dog's snout and across its back, claws ripping soft dog flesh, the cat made a tactical retreat towards the nearest high object – a post roughly tamped into the ground, at the top of which was a lit oil lamp.

Whoever had originally put up the post to hang a lamp from had never thought it might be used as an escape route by a fair-sized cat being chased by some enraged and frenzied dogs, one of whom would also attempt to climb it.

As the cat reached the top, the pole tilted and the

animal scrabbled to cling on; then the dog, the one with the bloodied nose, hit the pole as he leaped upwards to try and sink his teeth into his ginger tormentor, and the pole toppled over.

Ron and Mickey had been some yards away, watching with huge amusement the complete mayhem they'd wittingly caused. This, they both agreed, was the bestest cat'n'dog fight ever in the whole world, no doubt about it. But then it all suddenly changed. The lamp hit the ground and broke as it fell over, spilling oil onto a nearby bale of hay, oil which the wick immediately lit. Suddenly there was a huge amount of light, a great flare of yellow-to-red flames hungrily licking away the blackness of the night, and then chocking billows of smoke as the straw burned up and the fire took hold.

The boys stopped laughing and began screaming for help.

Daniel had taken no notice of the growling and screeching and barking. He had a good idea who was responsible for it, had thought it quite funny the first time he'd seen some mangy old thing tearing in a panic up the side of a caravan or a tent with a few of the dogs in hot pursuit. Now he was just tired to the bone and he wanted nothing more than to fall into his bed. Then he heard yelling, with a note of panic in the voices.

But it was the smoke in the air that stopped him dead in his tracks.

The bitter, acrid smell caught in the back of his throat and he could hardly believe it was really happening...there *couldn't* be a fire in the circus! More than anything he wanted to ignore that he'd ever seen those pictures in his head and carry on imagining that it had never happened, imagining that he was just like everyone else. Only there was a fire. Forcing himself to move, Daniel turned back and looked at the red glow he knew in his heart would be there.

The fire looked somehow smaller than what he'd seen in his head and he began sprinting towards it, realizing as he ran that it must be over where the horses were tethered for the night. Where Savage was tied up and unable to get away! The thought spurred him on, but as he ran the slower the going got; there were so many other people taking the same narrow pathways between caravans, mothers hurriedly shushing children away from the conflagration; others, like him, desperate to do something to help put the fire out.

Finally making his way through, Daniel came into the cramped space where the fire was raging, the intense heat pulling air in like a gale to feed the flames greedily eating anything they could reach. This was everyone's nightmare. Torrential rain or bone-chilling cold, hail storms or heatwaves, nothing could destroy the close-knit life of the travelling circus like fire.

Daniel was greeted by the sight of Sticky Jack's wife, lit by the blaze. Just as he'd seen, she was throwing a sodden horse blanket over a burning pile of straw. Then, to his right, he saw Billy Jiggs, a dark blue kerchief tied over his nose and mouth, run through the smoke towards where he knew the horses were tethered before being taken out into the temporary paddock for the night. Without a second's thought, he went after him. Keeping low, Daniel held his breath, half-closed his eyes and got through the worst of the smoke, coming out into slightly clearer air, hacking and wiping tears away from his eyes.

"Daniel! What in the name of all the saints are you doing here? Hannah'd climb a wall if she knew!"

Daniel looked up and saw Billy pulling the dampened blue cloth down off his nose. "I came to help, to get Savage and the rest out!"

"We ain't moving the horses."

"Why?" Daniel could hear the panicked whinnying, the nervous stamping of hooves. "What're we doing then?"

"Keeping 'em calm, making sure they don't make more trouble'n we've already got by breaking loose –

they've got a handle on the fire now, all they got to do is make sure it don't spread."

Daniel turned and looked behind him; a light wind had come up and through the thinning smoke he could see shadowy figures passing buckets, others using shovels to stamp out embers, and he could see that it looked like there was already more smoke than there was flame. He felt a sense of relief flood through him. "What started it?"

"Those idiot boys an' their catch-cat game."

"Ron 'n' Mickey?"

"Aye, them two...what's going to think their own backsides're on fire, mark my words, once they've felt the leather of their fathers' belts."

Daniel was just about to go over to the horses and find out how Savage was when a call went up behind him and he turned to see that the flames had taken hold again. It looked as if the fire, like the wily fox it was, had managed to find more fuel and the canvas of a small tent had caught alight. And Daniel could feel that the wind, which had changed direction, was blowing the flames towards him and Billy and the horses.

"We're going to have to move 'em now, Billy!"

"Looks that way." Billy pulled his kerchief up again. "You get in there and get Savage and Snowdrop out 'n' away first."

Daniel didn't wait to be told a second time. Moving down the line of tethered, skittering horses he made low, calming noises even though he could feel his own panic rising like bile from his stomach. It was as if he was being played with. One moment it all looked almost like a storm in a teacup and nothing really to worry about, and the next...he didn't want to think about what might happen next.

Reaching where Savage and Snowdrop were tied up, he moved between them, feeling their nervousness and tension. "I'm here...don't fret, I'm here," he crooned as he pulled at the reins, undid them and started to coax the horses to step backwards so he could lead them away from the smoke and fire. "Move back...slowly now, slowly..."

Around him he could see and hear the other horses, catching the reflection of the flickering orange light in their fearful eyes. Urging his two mounts forward into a trot, he ran with them away to the rear of the site, stopping only when he reached the paddock area; tying them to one of the posts he ran back into the muddle of tents and wagons, almost at once meeting Billy and Jem, who between them looked like they'd brought out at least six horses.

"I've tethered my two up the back – how many more left now? Is it four?"

"'Bout that..." Jem, black smuts marking his face, coughed and spat. "Got bad back there for a bit, be careful, the nags're fearsome jittery."

"Wait till I get back, Danny-boy..." Billy pulled down his kerchief, his face now divided into pale and soot-spattered. "It'll need the two of us."

"I'll go up and see what I can do, Billy," Daniel waved, "can't stand around and watch."

As he got closer to where the horses were tethered Daniel could hear the remaining beasts, their neighing eerily high-pitched. He knew they were going to be difficult to move in such a state; if he simply untied them and let them go they'd more than likely blunder wildly into something or someone, might even break a leg and have to be shot. There again, attempting to lead them out wasn't going to be the easiest of jobs.

Rounding a corner, Daniel saw that the fire was slowly being brought under control, but the wind was still sending red-hot embers flying into the air. The tiny glowing sparks, like red-hot midges, fell through the clearing smoke, landing on the backs of the three remaining horses and tormenting them. Daniel knew his horses and it didn't take him too long to work out what he could do, what might work, if luck was with him. He knew, if he could get up on the middle horse,

Ranger, while still holding the reins of the other two, he had a chance of controlling all three and getting them away to safety. But if he didn't do it quick he could see something bad was going to happen.

Moving forward, ignoring the stinging on his arms and hands and face from the bits of burning straw, he called out in his commanding voice, "Ranger! Here Ranger!" and waved to get the horse's attention. All three animals were by now frantic, eyes wide and pulling on their reins. It was now or never.

Daniel ducked under the wooden bar the horses were tethered to, praying that the animals, who all knew him well, wouldn't lose control completely and kick the life out of him. "I'm here, I'm going to get you out of here boys, going to get you out..." He took his bone-handled lock knife out of his pocket, opened it and gripped it, blade out, between his teeth.

Breathing as deep as he dared in the smoky air, he grabbed the centre and left-hand pair of reins in his right hand and untied them; dodging between Ranger and the other horse he jumped, using Ranger's mane to help pull him up onto his back. Sitting up he gripped hard with his knees, holding the pair of reins tightly wrapped round his fist, wrestling to keep the horses from dashing off. Taking the knife out of his mouth he leaned down as far as he could, slashed the other horse's reins, dropping the knife and grabbing at the flying strands of leather.

He caught one of the two and pulled sharply on it as a gust of wind blew a fresh rain of sparks at them. Feeling it was free, the third horse wanted to go – go anywhere as quickly as it could – and Daniel knew Ranger was the key to this working. If he could control him, keep him calm, the other two might follow his lead; he leaned forward. "Step, Ranger!" he commanded. "Step one-two! Left, right, left, right!"

All the horses could do this trick, march like they were in a rank of soldiers, it was something they were taught right from the beginning and Daniel could feel Ranger responding. "Step one-two! Left, right!" In the middle of all the chaos habit overcame the horses' panic, automatically making them follow orders, obey the commands to step at a measured pace, line abreast.

As they came running back from tethering the other horses, Jem and Billy could hardly believe their eyes when they saw Daniel marching the remaining horses away from the fire as if they were leaving the ring after a performance.

"Would you look at that!" Jem grinned, coming round to the side. "Here, gimme one of 'em."

"You all right, Danny-boy?" Billy held his hand out.

"I'll take the other two, you go and get yerself a drink of water."

"I'm fine...what about you two? How's Savage?"

"We're Jim-dandy, and so's all the horses, so come off there and let me finish this up."

Daniel swung down off Ranger, and handed over the reins, feeling exhaustion creep over him. "I'll get a drink and then come back, check on Savage."

"You do that, Danny-boy."

Watching Billy and Jem lead the horses away, Daniel swung the cord attached to his belt and caught his knife; unlocking the blade and folding it back, he put it in his pocket. As he walked off to find some water he found himself wondering what use it was seeing things that were going to happen if you couldn't do anything about them. Comus had said not to worry about having the visions – which was easy for him to say, as he wasn't the one having these terrible dreams. And he'd also said that the best protection was prevention, but it seemed to Daniel as if he couldn't even do that.

# CHAPTER 10
# THE BAG MEN

Tired and in something of a daze, Daniel wasn't really paying attention to where he was going, in the back of his mind thinking he should try and find Hannah. What he wanted as much as a drink of water was the comfort of being around someone who would look after him; he was scared, jittery, like the horses had been, and afraid of the things that were happening to him.

With the fire under control the campsite seemed to

be gradually settling back down. As he walked, Daniel saw small children being led off to their beds and a wave of exhaustion flooded over him; he was bone tired and saw his own fatigue mirrored in the faces of the men wiping their blackened hands with soaped cloths, of the people standing round discussing the events.

He heard snatches of conversation, nodded to those who waved at him, noticed how carefully those smoking put out their matches. The smell of burning hung in the air, the taste in every breath he took, and Daniel caught the pungent aroma of singed hair, taking a moment to realize it was coming from him.

Tired and slightly disoriented, he stopped for a moment to get his bearings, and saw that he was right by Josie Finnister's caravan, the one called Rosalie, when he heard his name being called. He looked round and there she was.

"You all right, Daniel? You look lost."

Daniel thought for a moment. "Tuckered, Josie...I'm tuckered and I'm thirsty."

"I'll get you a drink." Josie gently took his arm and guided Daniel up the steps and into her caravan, stopping at the door to turn up the oil lamp, painting the tiny interior with yellow light and dark, impenetrable shadows. "Sit down, I've water in the jug."

Daniel did as he was told, yawning and rubbing his eyes as he looked round at where he was, taking in the colourful rag carpets covering the floor, the lace trim on the white curtains drawn across the windows and the way the lamplight made Josie's hair shine. He leaned an elbow on the table next to him, then rested his head in his hand; by the time Josie had found a tin mug, filled it with water and turned to give it to him, Daniel was fast asleep.

Josie put the mug down. "Poor lad..." She went over and drew back the hanging cloth that curtained off her bed. "I'll lay you down while I go and get your Billy to come fetch you..."

Jacob Husker pulled out his polished steel hunter and flipped up the cover, turning the watch's white enamel face towards the candle still burning on the table. Near enough half past two of a moonless night, and one that would hopefully stay that way. Jacob closed his watch and tucked it back into his waistcoat pocket thinking that, once this job was over, maybe he'd treat himself to a new watch, a silver one like a proper gentleman would have. He'd be able to afford it.

Reaching down, he picked up one of his boots and lobbed it at Dooley, who was sprawled in the chair snoring, head lolled to one side, mouth open and dribbling. The ideal person to be sharing a room in a country inn with.

"Wake up, you lazy snot-gobbet!"

The boot hit Dooley's shoulder and he jerked awake with a loud snort, sliding off the chair and landing on the floor. "Wha...? What y'do that for?"

"Because I'm a man of me word, Aitch...now get up, pass me back me boot and let's be off."

Hampton Dooley reined in the horse and guided it off the track, bringing the brougham to a halt in the same place they'd left it earlier. Jumping down, he tied the horse to the nearest tree and then hobbled it for good measure; no sense in taking chances, like Jake always said.

Husker got out of the carriage, reaching back inside for a large sackcloth bundle that was tied up with thin, little finger-width rope. "Got the sap, Aitch?"

Dooley stood up, reached into his pocket and pulled out a sand-filled black woollen sock, knotted at the top, and swung the makeshift cosh left and right. "I wet it before we left."

"Only use it if we have to, all right? You could snap the girl's neck with that thing, and we won't get nothing for a body what ain't breathing."

"Reckon nobody'll be up now?"

Husker set off towards the field where the circus was pitched. "Surely do."

A few minutes later he was having to re-evaluate his opinion as he and Dooley stood in the trees, watching two figures they'd just seen meet, exchange a few words and carry on walking round the perimeter of the encampment. Both were carrying what looked to be pretty hefty cudgels.

"They've put a guard up, Jake."

"I can see that..." Husker grimaced, chewing his lower lip as he checked his watch, wondering if his crossing paths with that tricksy little girl had anything to do with this turn of events. "And keep yer voice down, eh?" This certainly complicated matters, but that was all...they'd just have to be more careful. Husker looked at his watch again. He wanted to see how long it took the two men to do their circuit.

Dooley took out the sock, heavy with dampened sand, and slapped it with a dull thud into the palm of his left hand. "Maybe I should do 'em both, next time they come round."

Husker glanced sideways at his companion. "Know what, Aitch? Maybe you should..."

It had worked a treat. The next time the men – boys really, as it turned out – had passed each other, the two conspirators had slipped across the scrub grass and hidden themselves, waiting for their chance. When the lookouts had come by again they'd stopped, one of them lighting a pipe from a match held by the other, and Dooley was there in a flash, silent as a cat after a mouse. Husker had to admit, dull as he might be in so many ways, he was a delight to watch in others.

It had taken only moments, just two swift, accurate taps and the boys were down; stowed well out of the way under some bushes, the two lads were going to wake up with the sorriest of heads, but at least now the coast was a lot clearer.

They crept between the silent caravans and tents and then Husker stopped, tapped Dooley on the shoulder, and pointed at the caravan he'd seen Josie come out of, the one that was called Rosalie. A smell of burning and damp ash lingered in the night air and Husker wondered to himself what had caused it. Since entering the camp neither of the men had uttered a word – and wouldn't until they were well away. From now on it was all sign language.

Undoing the knotted uneven length ropes tying up the bundle, Husker wound them round his fist and put one in each of his deep coat pockets; unrolling the bundle he shook it free to reveal a large sack, nearly six foot in length, with a couple of ties at the open end.

It gave off a decidedly musty odour and felt damp to the touch.

Husker nodded Dooley forward to the steps of the caravan. Boots on the outside edges, to lessen the likelihood of the steps squeaking, Dooley crept up to the door and stopped. Quickly checking around him, he took a small oil can out of his coat pocket, unscrewed the cap off its thin nozzle and dripped some of the contents on the hinges and the latch.

He glanced at Husker, who waited a moment or two, listening, then nodded. Dooley lifted the latch, pulled the door open and stepped inside. Husker followed, silently closing the door behind him.

Inside it was pitch-dark, like being blindfolded, but it was going to have to stay that way. Standing inches apart, waiting for the time it took for their eyes to adapt, the two men breathed as quietly as they could as they looked round the tiny space. Slowly, very slowly, they began to make out shapes. What they did in the next few minutes was going to have to happen fast, with little room for error; Husker made out the hunched form a few feet away, lying on what must be the bed, put the sack down and gave a thumbs up.

They'd done quite a few jobs like this before and Dooley stepped forward in a practised move, scooping the sleeping figure up off the bed, blanket and all, his left hand clamped over its mouth. The girl felt light as a feather, and Dooley could smell her lavender perfume, warm as it came off her.

Husker pulled a yard-long piece of rope out of one of his coat pockets, kneeled and tied it round the figure's ankles; he could do this kind of thing with his eyes closed, which was lucky as he could hardly see his hands in front of his face. He stood up and from a trouser pocket he took out a couple of kerchiefs and tapped his partner's shoulder. Dooley turned to face him and moved his hand away from their victim's mouth; as he did so Husker stuffed one kerchief in and tied the other round the head.

Dropping the figure face down on the bed, Dooley stood back as his partner tied a longer piece of rope around its torso. Bending down he picked up the sack, handing it over as soon as he saw in the gloom that Husker had finished tying the knot; he then lifted the trussed-up body again. Husker opened the sack and Dooley slid their now squirming, but silent quarry inside. The moment the sack was tied Dooley bent down slightly, dropped it over one shoulder, stood up and squinted at Husker.

Motioning Dooley forward to wait by the door, Husker was about to do a quick search for the girl's bag, as he'd been instructed, when he heard voices outside the caravan. They were somewhere in the distance, but still too close for comfort. The choice was to spend precious seconds feeling about in the dark for something which could be anywhere, or get out while the going was good, which, as a man of his profession knew, was no choice at all. The girl on her own would have to do.

Husker signalled to Dooley that he should go, so he opened the door and went gingerly down the steps, a firm grip on the sack on his shoulder. By the time Husker closed up the caravan, they had been inside it no more than two minutes. Three minutes later they were at the edge of the camp and about to make for the trees when they heard more voices.

"They should've woke me 'n' you, right? Not let us come to find 'em... Where are they anyway?"

"Dunno."

"They wouldn't've sneaked off, would they?"

"Nowhere to sneak off to, is there?"

From their hiding place behind a wagon, Husker watched two youths wander past in search of their friends. Any moment now they were going to start calling their names, and that was going to make life more problematic as it was bound to bring out more people with lamps and prying eyes.

*They were at the edge of the camp*
*and about to make for the trees.*

Should he risk sending Dooley to sap them? Or should he wait till they were out of sight? Weighing everything up, Husker signalled Dooley, standing behind him with Josie – his passage to New York – over his shoulders, to wait where he was. She was wriggling like a worm on a hook, a feisty one, that girl, and no mistake. She would have to be, mused Husker, to want to get on the wrong side of Carter Bland.

Then the coast was clear, no one in sight.

Husker waved his hand forward and made a run for it, Dooley, with his little lady passenger, coming after him. They went past the bushes where they'd hidden the two boys, across the last of the open ground and on towards the safety of the trees. If their luck held, they'd be on the road, London-bound, in no time.

# CHAPTER 11
# MISSING!

If there was no early start the next day, it was James Hubble's habit to drink, smoke and play cards until he fell asleep or dawn broke, whichever event occurred first. It was also his habit to insist Comus stayed up with him, and tonight he'd called Josie in as well, although she'd left ten minutes ago now. Tired, she'd said, and maybe that was true.

Comus didn't mind as he enjoyed these times with Hubble, this paradoxical, contradictory man who could be the accomplished showman in the ring – so skilled at keeping an audience entranced and entertained – as well as the man outside of the tent; the stern, grumpy, sometimes sour person, more given to the glower than the smile, so different to the face he showed to the crowds. What amazed Comus was that these two sides were able to live within the same person, the man of simple pleasures and fierce loyalty he was proud to call his friend.

One of the many reasons he liked to stay up with Hubble was that he'd found, as he got older, that he needed less sleep and, because he never drank as much as his friend; he also won more than he lost in the card games.

"We were lucky tonight, eh, Bruise?"

"We? What d'you mean 'we'?" Hubble tapped his glass on the table and then knocked back the finger of brandy it contained. "You won all the money, you and yer card-sharp ways..."

"I meant lucky there wasn't no one hurt in the fire."

"That we were, most certainly." Hubble belched loudly as he put his glass down and reached for the bottle to refill it. The smell of the fire was everywhere, clinging to hair and clothes like a bad dream that refused to go away, even when you woke; he shook his head as he brought his glass up for another sip. "Those boys..."

"I believe the little blockheads'll have learned a lesson, Bruise," Comus grinned. "And won't be sitting down much for a couple of days neither!"

"Nothing less than they deserve...been told before." Hubble put the glass to his lips, but was interrupted by the door to his caravan being flung open before he could take a drink. Both men turned, quizzical expressions on their faces, to see Josie Finnister standing outside, white as a sheet.

Hubble put his glass down. "Josie?"

Comus stood up. "Lord, what is it girl?"

"Daniel..."

"What about him?"

"He's not there, Comus...we went...Billy and me, we went to get him and he wasn't there." Josie, looking distraught, hugged herself like she had a pain in her stomach.

"Wasn't where?" Hubble looked across the table at his friend, puzzled. "Where the Hell should the boy be at this time of the night but in his bed?"

Comus stepped over and brought Josie into the caravan, sitting her on the spare chair at the table. "Why'd you and Billy have to go anywhere for Daniel, girl?" Comus nodded at Hubble, pointing to the brandy bottle on the table. "Pour her a glass of yer bingo, she looks like she could do with a sip."

"He was asleep in Rosalie... I found him, just after the fire, looking tired and not himself, saying he wanted a drink of water." Josie glanced from one man to the other. "But he fell asleep before I could give it him, see, so I laid him down...I was going to go straight to fetch Billy, but got sidetracked when you two called me in here for a game and glass or two... I forgot, didn't I, Bruise? I forgot and now he's gone."

"Maybe he's woke and is on his way back to his own bed." Comus patted Josie's arm and gave her the brandy Hubble had poured. "Or even sleepwalking, could be sleepwalking."

"Billy's out checking now, but..." Josie put the glass down untouched and took a deep breath, biting her knuckle.

"But what?" Hubble leaned forward.

"It was me they were after, Bruise...sure as eggs it was those two men Comus saw – they came back, I know they did!"

"How so?"

"There was a smell in the caravan...it was damp, like an old cellar, and that little place wasn't smelling like that when I left Daniel there. Them two came back and they made a mistake and took Daniel instead." In front of their eyes the two men saw Josie crumple like the bones had been taken out of her, tears running down her cheeks as she sobbed. "I should've gone for Billy straight away, not sat here jawing till all hours...he shouldn't've been there..."

"There's no blame, Josie, no blame." Comus pulled a kerchief that had once been white out of one of his pockets and handed it to her. "Tell her, Bruise."

Josie sat up, sniffing and wiping away the tears with the back of her hand. "If I hadn't've ran away here, Carter Bland wouldn't've sent those men after me. Whatever you say, this is all my fault and that's the truth of it."

"We don't know it was him...might not be." Comus shrugged.

"Who else could it be?"

"You saw him tonight, Josie, he's a real crowd-puller is Daniel."

"So?"

"So someone might be trying to nobble him."

Josie gave Comus a withering look. "Don't try and soft-soap me and tell me tales. This is Carter Bland's work and you know I'm right about that."

She sat up straighter and took a deep breath; the colour returned to her cheeks as she pushed her despair and fright away and looked over at Hubble. "That man's a bad lot, Bruise, as bad as they come... and the people what work for him are no better, with some I've met being a lot worse. When they find out they haven't got me, Lord only knows what they'll do."

Comus glanced at Hubble, waiting to see what his friend was going to say, but Josie stood up and carried on talking.

"I'll have to go back to the Smoke...go now, as soon as possible, straight to The Ace and give myself up to Bland, tell him to let the boy go. Can you give me the use of a trap and a driver?"

Before Hubble could reply, Billy Jiggs appeared at the caravan's open door, out of breath and looking frantic. "No sign, Josie..."

Josie bit her lip and didn't say anything; she looked from Billy to Mr. Hubble, who stood up, swaying only slightly.

"You double-sure you checked *every*where?"

"Didn't have to, Mr. Hubble."

"And why the blue blazes not?"

"Ned and Mattie were just found, knocked silly and laid under some bushes...Sy and George went looking for 'em when they didn't come to get 'em to take over the rounds." Billy looked directly at Mr. Hubble. "Someone's been in the camp, no doubt about that, come in by owl-light and took Daniel with 'em when they left. What're we going a'do?"

Hubble stood by the table, still and silent as a rock, not looking anywhere in particular.

You might imagine that he was asleep with his eyes open, Comus thought, but he knew you'd be wrong. He was making plans, doing that thing of his, of holding his own counsel and only speaking when he knew what he was going to say. Also, his thinking would be a bit slower, on account of he'd been drinking.

Outside the caravan, behind Billy, Comus could see there was a small crowd of people gathering, mostly the boys who'd been patrolling. Then he saw Hannah, a dark shawl wrapped tight round her shoulders, come into the light.

"Where is he, Mr. Hubble, sir?"

Comus moved to the door. "We don't know, Hannah."

Hannah pointed through the open doorway. "What was he doing in her caravan, tell me that?"

People had gathered round Hannah, murmuring, and heads were nodding in agreement; Comus saw Josie, who'd kept her back to the door, turn and start to stand up. Before she could, Hubble moved in front of her.

"This stops right this very minute, you hear?" The crowd visibly shrank back. "There is no blame to be laid, no fault to be owned up to. What has happened is a mistake and the result of circumstance, not negligence, and if I hear anyone say otherwise they'll be out of my circus on their ear and never welcome back. We look after our own in this world, and Josie's a part of the family, no more to be said."

It was a measure, Comus knew, of how much Billy and Hannah felt for Daniel that while others began to fade away they stayed where they were.

"But what're we going a'do, Mr. Hubble, sir?"

"You, Billy, are going to stay here and, with the help of every able-bodied man, woman and child, you and Comus here are going to keep this circus on the road till I get back from London with Daniel." Hubble nodded, as if agreeing with himself. "That's what you'll be doing."

Once everybody had gone, Josie closed the caravan's door, came back to sit at the table and reached for the glass of brandy still waiting for her. "You can't do anything about Carter Bland, Bruise, he's too rich and too powerful for the likes of us." She took a sip, and made a grimacing face. "Call this brandy?"

"Call it what you like, missy; it keeps me as well as I can expect."

"Just let me go by my own…all he wants is me. I go back, he gets what he wants and he'll let Daniel go."

Comus finished preparing his pipe and lighting it. "I

don't wish to sound a disagreeable note, but what's he going to do, this Carter Bland, when he finds out those two we're assuming took Daniel got the wrong person? Ain't going t'be too happy, I'd say."

Josie drank the rest of the brandy in a gulp, pursing her lips as it went down. "He'll use him as a lure to get me to come back, is what he'll do Comus, so I may as well save him the trouble."

"And you know full well, Josie, that walking back into The Ace is like signing your own death warrant and putting your head in the hangman's noose." Hubble took a pinch of snuff. "He knows you heard him with that man, that perfidious Russian, he knows you took them papers. He's going to want you dead, Josie, no more, no less."

"But what else can I do?" A single tear welled up and ran down her cheek as Hubble took a second pinch and smiled. "This ain't no laughing matter, Bruise!"

"Never said it was."

"Now he's got Daniel I'm lost..."

"You've no reason to think like that, girl." Hubble got out his pocket knife and opened up the blade; taking a spent match off the table he proceeded to sharpen the used end and then pick his back teeth with it.

Josie watched and waited for a moment, expecting to hear the grounds for why she shouldn't think the way she was, but none were seemingly forthcoming. "Why, Bruise?"

"Why what, girl?"

"Why isn't everything lost now Bland's got Daniel – how else can it be?"

"A'coz the cove is acting desperate, that's why."

"He is?"

"Certainly."

Josie looked at Comus, who shrugged. "For the sake of my sanity, will you *please* tell me what you're thinking and what we're goin' to do!"

"More brandy?" Hubble offered Josie the bottle, smiling, and she looked at him fit to spit. "Fine, just asking, girl..."

Comus, who'd been watching the exchange between Hubble and Josie, leaned forward and tapped his pipe on the table. "Pardon me, but I ain't got a clue what the two of you're blabbing on about."

Hubble sat back in his chair. "Did I not tell you?" Comus shook his head. "I was sure I had...well, you know we've been at war with them Russians over in the Crimea for a year and some such now, don't you?"

"I may be older'n the hills, but I'm not a numbskull; last I heard, some feller was telling me they've had Sebastopol under siege for nigh on eleven month now."

"True enough...well, Josie's Mr. Bland, he's been dealing with them Russians on the sly, making a lot of dishonest pennies doing business with our enemies. Long and the short of it, right, Josie?"

Comus scratched his bald head. "How d'you know all this, Josie?"

"I was going over to The Ace a week or so ago – coming in the back way, like we have to, us who aren't paying customers. Like I told Bruise, it was very early, the place was empty, no one about that I could see, and I was going up the back stairs to Mr. Bland's rooms on the second floor. I'd just opened the door on to the corridor when I heard a blazing row, so I stayed back on the landing, kept the door ajar and I heard every word of it.

"Mr. Bland was angry, talking like it was to a child to this man called...it sounded more or less like Nakhimov. Him, the foreigner, was yelling back – '*You made deal! You promise to deliver!*'" Josie mimicked a heavy, curt accent. "'*My fazzer pay you for guns, not excuses!*' – like that, and Bland was telling him to keep his voice down, that there'd been some problems, but everything he'd ordered would be through the family's warehouses in the next few days and en route to Riga, he said, just like the other shipments.

"I read the newspapers," Josie glanced at Comus, "I realized the man must be a Russian, and he wasn't best pleased, said the war could be over before what he'd paid for arrived."

"How long did you stay?"

"Too long, Comus. I should've went, but I knew what I was hearing was important. And then the Russian stormed out, shouting at Bland and Bland was following him down the corridor, yelling back." Josie turned to Hubble. "I don't know why I went in, Bruise, I really don't know what come over me, but I kept on thinking I might find something in there. I could hear Bland, bellowing at the other man as he went down the front stairs, so I nipped out the door, into his rooms and took the papers that were on his desk – official-looking letters and such, with ribbons and wax seals."

"How'd Bland find out, did he see you?"

"No, he was still down the end of the corridor, yelling, when I come out. It was Queenie saw me, Comus."

"Queenie?"

"Mr. Bland's mother...that's what we call her; she must've been the only other person in the place, and she saw me coming down the back stairs. I still had the papers in my hand and she asked me what I was doing."

"And you ran."

Josie nodded. "Like a hare...had just enough money

on me to take a growler back to The Sun, packed a small bag and left."

"And now that everyone knows everything," Hubble stood up and stretched, "you go and pack that bag again, Josie, I'll go and rouse Sam Baston and the three of us'll be on our way to London."

"Hold on...what about the papers?" Comus was frowning. "What were they?"

"No idea, they were all in Russian, or some such...could've been Greek for all the sense they made to me."

"You got 'em with you?"

"No, I stashed them in my room at The Sun, there's a loose floorboard right under the bed...thought they'd be safer there. No doubt Bland thinks they're with me, though." Josie glanced at Hubble. "What's your plan then, Bruise, once we get to London?"

"Revenge, Josie. Bland has come here and took Daniel." Frowning, Hubble stared at the scarred tabletop, nodding to himself while Comus and Josie waited for him to continue; when he looked up his face was still as a painting, except for a twitch in his left eye. "He may not be my blood, and I might not be what fancier folk would think of as any kind of father, but he's all the son I've got and will ever have. And make no mistake, I am going to get him back..."

## CHAPTER 12

# THE COLD LIGHT OF DAY

Jacob Husker sat in the brougham, Dooley up front, keeping the horse at a fair pace for the state of the road they were travelling. On the seat next to him, still in the sack, Josie Finnister was slumped against the side of the coach. Not quite worth her weight in gold, but nonetheless, a very valuable little package. He patted what he assumed was probably her knee and Josie, who'd been still as a mouse so far, but for the shaking and bouncing of the carriage, flinched.

It was, by his watch, now almost an hour since they'd left the outskirts of Marlborough and Dooley'd been making good time. They must be four, maybe even five miles gone now and dawn was beginning to break. With luck and only a couple of short stops along the way to rest, feed and maybe change the horse, they'd be back in the Smoke not so long after midnight. They might well have been able to do the journey somewhat quicker by railway, but not with a young lady bound and gagged and tied up in a sack like an unwanted kitten. Husker smiled to himself. Except this particular kitten was very much the opposite of unwanted.

Maybe now would be a good time to let the girl get some fresh air. He'd keep her gagged, just let her breathe a bit easier, no point in making her life a complete misery. He'd leave that to Carter Bland. Husker pulled the blinds down on the door windows, just in case of prying eyes, then reached over and began working loose the knot which held the sack closed; pulling the two ends of the cord apart he opened the neck of the sack and let it fall.

"Jeesus-Mary-mother-a...DOOLEY! Dooley pull up and stop!" Husker leaned forward and rapped on the glass at the front of the brougham with his knuckles. He saw Dooley look back over his shoulder, frowning. "I said pull up man, *pull up!*"

As the coach slowed Husker looked over at the face peering back at him in the early morning light. Out of the corner of his eye he saw Dooley rein in the horse, apply the brake and then jump down from the driver's seat. Turning round, Husker opened the carriage door and stepped down onto the road.

"What is it, Jake? You taken ill?"

"Have a glim inside."

"She's not died, 'as she?"

"Just take a look."

Dooley cocked his head and peered over Husker's shoulder; glancing, puzzled, at his companion, he went to the brougham's door. Leaning forward Dooley stuck his head in, the sight reminding Husker of a curious, mangy chicken, and jerked back out again.

"Th'ain't her, Jake..."

"No, it surely ain't."

"That's a lad."

"Correct."

"Well damn my eyes..." Dooley took his hat off and shook his head as he scratched his thinning scalp.

"Damn 'em indeed, Aitch old son, damn them indeed."

"She play some kind of tricksy game on us, Jake?"

"How could she know we was coming then, eh?" Husker stood, rubbing his chin, a blank expression on his face. "She couldn't've..."

"Who couldn't've what, Jake?"

"That..." Husker was about to mention the little girl who'd tripped him up, but thought better of making Dooley aware of that particular circumstance, realizing that the child could well be the reason everything seemed to have gone west.

"It was the right caravan we went into, wos'nit?"

Husker swung round. "Rosalie – you saw it said Rosalie, painted above the door!"

"If you say so, Jake."

"Well on my life – and may I be struck down – it did..." Husker felt like he'd been punched in the stomach as the full implications of what had happened sunk in. No Josie, no money; no money, no future for Jacob Husker across the Atlantic. His world, like a house of cards, was teetering on the point of collapse.

"What're we going to do?"

His partner's voice brought Husker back and made his brain, stuck solid and seemingly unable to cope with what was happening, start working once again. "What's Mr. Bland going to do, more's the question, Dooley... what is Mr. Bland going to do?"

"Who is he anyway?"

"Who?"

"The boy what ain't Josie Finnister."

"Pull him over and take the gag out...let's ask the little blighter."

Dooley stepped up into the back of the coach and heaved the sack over towards the door. Stepping back down, he untied the gag. "It's that boy what rode the horses, Jake. I'd lay money down."

His jaw aching from being gagged, Daniel licked his dry lips and looked from one man to the other, finally settling his gaze on Husker as he stepped a little closer. "Who the Hell are you, boy? And what were you doing in that caravan, tonight of all nights?"

Daniel took a deep breath and looked away, reacting as if everything that had just been said to him had been spoken in a language he'd never heard before.

"Maybe he's dumb-fogged, Jake. Lost his tongue from fright."

"Maybe he is, but he don't appear too scared to me." Husker reached out and grabbed Daniel's dirty face, smeared with whatever it was the sack had last been used to carry; he squeezed his cheeks hard as he turned Daniel so he had to look at him. "Name, boy...give us your moniker or I'll tan yer skinny backside."

"Daniel...my name's Daniel."

"Well, Daniel," Husker let go of his face, wiping his hands on his trousers, "tell me why you ain't Josie Finnister?"

"Can I have a drink?"

Husker reached out and slapped the side of Daniel's head. "Don't cheek me, boy; I'll think about wetting your whistle after I get some answers. Why were you in that p'tickler caravan?"

"Fell asleep...after the fire. Josie must've left me."

"What fire?"

"There was a fire, last night...an accident."

Husker, remembering the smell in the air as they approached Josie's caravan, nodded. "So...she, Josie, never put you up to this?"

Daniel shook his head. "Don't know what you mean."

Dooley pushed back the sleeves of his coat. "Want me to hit him this time, Jake?"

"No."

"Why not?"

Husker cracked all his knuckles, one by one. "'Cos I don't think he's lying to me."

"Can I hit him anyway, for not being Josie?"

"No."

"But..."

"Will you shut your gob for one moment, I'm *trying* to think..."

Daniel watched the two men. The smaller one, the one with the slight limp a bit like Billy's – Jake, the other man had called him – was the boss, that much was obvious. As was the fact that it had been Josie they'd come for. They were the people Mr. Hubble had told him were looking for her because she had taken something they wanted. No doubt about it.

And now they'd got him instead.

A shiver ran down Daniel's spine, part fear of what would become of him, part early morning chill. He was finding it hard to make sense of what had happened, as the last thing he remembered was sitting at the small table in Josie's caravan, waiting for her to get him some water (which he could *really* do with now).

And then, like one of his bad, bad dreams, everything got turned upside down. It must've been the big man who'd grabbed him, gripping him tight round the chest, a hand over his mouth and nose. That moment, when he'd woken suddenly from a deep, deep sleep, Daniel had, for a fleeting moment, thought he was drowning. Then he'd felt himself being gagged and tied up. In the pitch-black, unable to see or move or cry out, he'd felt completely helpless, a sense made all the worse because neither of the people (even half asleep, he'd realized there was more than one person manhandling him) had spoken a word.

Glancing down at the rough weave of the filthy sack he was still mostly covered by, Daniel recalled the heavy, laboured breathing of the man holding him, the hot breath in his ear. He could still smell the alcohol and the tobacco and the sweat of the man, mingled with the earthy, vegetable odour of the sacking. When he'd first realized, slung over the man's shoulder like a rolled carpet, that he was being taken from the circus, he couldn't imagine why he was being kidnapped; now, watching the two conspirators, with the knowledge that it was Josie they really wanted, he wondered what they were going to do with him.

What was she doing stealing something so extremely valuable? Josie didn't, Daniel thought, look like a thief, and Mr. Hubble wasn't someone who had much time for what he called "the light-fingered brigade". With him it was always a fair day's work for a fair day's pay, and don't ever expect nothing for nothing. For him to be on such good terms as he seemed to be with Josie, she must be an honest person at heart. An honest person who had taken an article so precious and important she was worth kidnapping to get it back. Except they'd got him instead.

The small one, Jake, kept glancing at him as he walked up and down chewing his thumbnail; the bigger one had given up waiting to hear what his friend was thinking and Daniel could see him with the horse, checking the animal's tack. If he wasn't who Jake had expected when he opened up the sack, if he wasn't the person they'd been sent to get, what was likely to happen to him?

Nothing good, that was for sure. He would be worthless to them, fit only to be discarded like a spent match. The thought that he was probably going to end up, strangled, in some ditch caused another shiver to run down his spine, this one nothing at all to do with feeling cold.

But just sitting and waiting for his fate to be delivered to him seemed like a very bad way to spend what could be his last few minutes on Earth; even though escape was unlikely, Daniel felt he had to have a go...

The panic of a fire, followed by disturbances in the night *and* an early start, didn't make for even tempers and happy dispositions in Hubble's Circus. Added to which was the fact that – no two ways about it – Daniel had been kidnapped.

Josie could feel the anxiety and knew that much of the bad feeling was being directed at her, no matter what Bruise had said. Even though she had no wish to go back to London, she wanted nothing more right now than to get out of the circus and onto the road. Away. She wanted to be nowhere near the place if something had happened to Daniel – and well it might, once the men who'd taken him discovered they had the wrong person. Well it might.

Packing the last of her things into her old brown leather portmanteau and closing the two sides of the case, Josie waited for Bruise to come and get her. It'd taken some little time, but she'd managed to persuade him that taking the train would be the right thing to do. He'd been a hard man to convince, not given to what he called "newfangledness", or changing his mind once he'd made it up. While she knew the train was their best bet, getting them to London much quicker than if they went by road – the way the kidnappers would have to travel, given the "luggage" they were taking with them – she wasn't at all sure about Bruise's choice of travelling companion.

James Hubble Esq. was not someone you could ever miss in a crowd, but Sam Baston, all black-as-coal six foot or more of him, stood out even more. There was no way he was going to go unnoticed, she'd pointed out, but Bruise had been insistent. They weren't going to London to hide in the shadows like gutter-prowlers and finger-smiths, they were going there to make other people listen, he'd said, whether they liked it or not. And you didn't do that by being quiet. So, while Josie had won her argument over method of travel, she lost it concerning the third member of the team. Sam was coming, and that was that.

Lost in thought, wondering quite what they were going to do, once they got to London, Josie was brought back to reality by a knock on her caravan's door.

"Miss?"

"Yes?" Quickly looking round one last time, Josie picked up her bonnet. "Come in."

The door was opened by a young boy, a little older than Daniel, Josie thought his name was Seth.

"Come to get yer bags, miss... Mr. Hubble sent me as the wagon's ready, miss."

"Thank you, Seth...it is Seth, isn't it?"

"Yes, miss."

"Just the one bag, Seth." Josie nodded at the portmanteau on the table, remembering that it was where Daniel had fallen asleep, exhausted after the fire, and wondering if she'd ever see him alive again. She turned and went down the steps, out into the chill morning, and saw the pale-blue dawn sky chasing the last of the night away into the west.

# CHAPTER 13
# ON THE ROAD

"Right!"

Daniel, who'd been staring off into the middle distance as he tried, unsuccessfully, to surreptitiously move the rope around his middle so he could reach the knot, looked up; he saw the one called Jake rubbing his hands together, smiling, then the other man came into view.

"What's up, Jake?"

"Put the boy back up on the seat and let's be moving."

"Where to?"

"The Ace, Dooley, The Ace – back to London and step to it!"

Daniel relaxed slightly; they weren't going to kill him. Here, anyway. He watched the big man, Dooley, stay where he was, as if his feet were nailed down to the road. "London? What about that we haven't got Josie?"

"Come 'ere." Husker beckoned to Dooley, looking left and right like he was checking, out in the middle of nowhere, that no one could hear what he was about to say. "What would happen, say, if we was to've took this sack up to town and never have opened it? Left it tied up all the time, for safe keeping. Then, if we'd went in the back way, like we always do, gone up to Mr. Carter Bland's room and *that's* where we'd undone the rope, what would happen, Dooley?"

"Mr. Bland would spit fire, Jake. Just like he's going to."

"True, but it wouldn't be our fault, would it, 'cos we were tricked, right?" Husker winked at his partner. "And, see, *we* would be as took by surprise as him, wouldn't we? *If* we hadn't of opened the sack."

"But we '*ave* opened it, Jake...leastways, you did."

"He don't know that, Dooley...Mr. Bland does not *know* that. And if you don't tell him, neither will I."

"What about the boy, won't he say?"

Husker looked over at Daniel. "If he did, Mr. Bland

ain't going to believe some lying, filthy little gypsy boy over us." He sidled up to the brougham and leaned over Daniel. "And if he's got an ounce of wit he'll keep his domino box shut tight, won't you lad? Else you'll wish you'd never been born...never."

Quite why Husker did it Daniel wasn't sure, but, much to Daniel's surprise, the man let him sit on the seat, left him ungagged, took off the rope round his waist and pushed the sack down so it might look like his legs were covered with a blanket. Maybe, in that sneaky way some grown-ups had, he was being nice on the one hand – so Daniel wouldn't say anything to this Mr. Bland they were on their way to see – all the while leaving the threat hanging that he'd beat him senseless if he did. The answer came pretty soon.

"One uncalled-for peep out of you, boy, and you'll be back in the sack and down on the floor so fast you'll wonder how." Husker sat back and lit up a pipe. "But I believe you're a lad what has brains. If you do right by me, I'll do right by you. As right as I can, considering the circumstances."

Daniel frowned. "What can I do for you?"

"You'll play the game my way, lad, that's what you can do. And if you do, I won't let nothing bad happen to you. Husker's word."

Looking out of the carriage window, Daniel knew exactly how much a man like Husker's word was worth. Precious little, if anything. He was a villain and a chancer and he, like most people it seemed, had a low opinion of travellers...filthy little gypsy boy indeed! But any ally, even one you couldn't trust, was better than none at all. "I won't say anything, sir."

"A sensible decision."

"Who is Mr. Bland, anyway, and why does he want Josie Finnister bad enough to kidnap her? What's she done?"

"Not for me to know," Husker replied, sounding, thought Daniel, just like Comus.

Glancing at his captor, Daniel couldn't tell if he was lying or not and just left it. His head was filled with a jumble of thoughts and emotions and he knew he had to keep himself calm if he was to have any chance of working out what was going to happen to him, and what he was going to do to try and stop it.

His whole life he'd been trained to take chances, but only once he knew everything he could know about the situation. A trick on horseback only looked dangerous because the audience would never have the nerve to do it themselves, didn't know how and wouldn't trust themselves to get it right. They would believe they'd be bound to fail. Billy had schooled Daniel to believe he would succeed, but only if he knew his strengths and his limitations, and only if he pushed himself, but never pushed too far. The thing Billy hated most was any sign of the daredevil; the accident that had crippled him had been caused by someone chancing their arm, making a mistake and taking another person down with them.

Daniel understood, without even having to think about it, that there was no point in attempting to throw himself out of the carriage while it was moving. Although he knew how to fall so he'd land, and there'd hardly be a mark on him, with his feet still tied and legs wrapped in the sack he'd never get away. He'd get caught and achieve nothing but a beating. And if there was one lesson Billy had drummed into him it was that everything you did should have a purpose, should lead to something positive, and that the worst thing you could do was waste time.

Now, with nothing but time on his hands, Daniel reasoned that the best use of it was to fix into his memory as much as he could of what had happened since he'd been taken from Josie's caravan. Anything that might be of benefit if he managed to escape. All he'd really found out, though, were some names; the smaller man was Jake Husker, the larger one Dooley – he recalled Husker calling him Aitch – and the man who seemed to be behind all this was someone called Carter

Bland. The only other piece of information he had was his final destination, somewhere called The Ace. Whatever and wherever that was, only time would tell.

Not much to go on. Snippets, as Hannah would call them.

The thought of Hannah, the picture of her in his mind's eye, brought his train of thought to a dead halt and gave Daniel an almost physical pain – what would she be thinking, now that they must've discovered that he'd gone from the circus?

He couldn't remember when he didn't know the fact that he was an orphan, because the truth hadn't been hidden from him, but he'd never felt like one. Even though he'd never had a real mother, he'd grown up surrounded by plenty of families and he knew Hannah loved him like he was her own. She'd be going mad...

With almost no warning – perhaps just a slight tingling in the tips of his fingers – that strange, rather abrupt shift he'd experienced before, as if someone had unexpectedly changed the painted glass slide in a magic lantern show, occurred.

And then Daniel found himself somewhere else.

He was in a room, a small, dark room without any windows. In this place that looked like a cell, sitting hunched on a narrow mattress and looking very sorry for himself, was the one called Dooley. Suddenly, there was a loud explosion and the door to the room burst open and Husker rushed in holding a smoking pistol, angry and shouting something about how stupid Dooley was, letting a boy get the better of him. Dooley stood up and...

And that was when Daniel shifted again, back to the reality of sitting, tied up, in a coach taking him to London. He took a sharp breath and shot a puzzled glance at the man, Husker, sitting across the seat from him.

"Something wrong, boy? You look bone-white under all that grime."

"Just thirsty, sir."

"So we all are, and we'll all get some ale as soon as we stop for the horse."

Husker turned away and stared out of his side of the carriage, leaving Daniel to wonder what the scene he'd just witnessed could mean. He knew by now that the things he saw in these waking dreams had a habit of coming true, but witnessing events – someone who you'd heard was soon to arrive, seeing a fire, when fires were not an unknown hazard when you lived in a circus – was something he could almost convince himself, truly *wanted* to convince himself, was some kind of weird coincidence.

Seeing secret, unknown things was different.

Daniel looked sideways at Husker – what had *this* moment uncovered? He sat still, trying to work through his head what the scene meant, trying to unpick the significance of the few seconds of what must be, even though he didn't want to believe it, the future. Why he saw these things he had no idea, but he did know that it didn't frighten him any more, not like the first time. This wasn't something he had any control over, but it was something he was going to have to learn to live with. And also, why not, learn to use? He'd have to wait and see what his future really held.

For want of anything better to do, Daniel stared out of the carriage window at the passing countryside and then, some time later, glanced at his travelling companion, the silent Mr. Husker. It was as obvious as the nose on a gin drinker's face that, of the two, Jake Husker was the brains while the man up front was the muscle and Daniel wondered how much money they were getting for what they were doing.

"Do kidnappers get paid a lot?"

Husker did a double take. "What did you say?"

"Nothing..."

"Way this job's going we'll be lucky to get a bean." Husker shook his head as he cracked his knuckles. "And who knows what'll happen to you..."

* * *

Daniel woke with a start, jolted out of his deep sleep as one of the brougham's wheels hit a substantial pothole and lurched sideways, sending him flying across the seat and into Husker's lap.

"You taking forty winks up there, Aitch!" Husker yelled, pushing Daniel off him and straightening his hat. "That hole must've been big enough to bury a blasted dog in!"

"Reckon a drain collapsed, more'n likely," Dooley shouted back over his shoulder, lit like a ghost by the carriage's two oil lamps.

"Just watch it, will you?"

"I'll watch you, squire!" Dooley reached behind him and banged the glass with his fist. "Don't get all high 'n' mighty with me – come up here, see how you do."

Daniel looked out of the window; it was pitch-black and he had no idea how long he'd been asleep. "What time is it, sir?"

Husker glanced at him, then pulled out his watch and inspected the face. "Thirty some minutes after twelve midnight." He snapped the cover shut and fed the shiny metal case back into his waistcoat pocket. "We'll be there shortly."

"Where?"

"I wouldn't be too eager, boy, not in your place. You'll find out, soon enough."

Daniel knew London reasonably well, at least the parts where the circus played, and knew it a lot better over in the east of town, where they wintered, but he couldn't recognize anything that would give him a clue as to where they were now. Or where they might end up. At intervals, pools of hazy gaslight illuminated the route they were travelling on, the carriage moving at a decent pace along the cobbled streets, the horse's hooves and the iron-rimmed wheels loud on the stone, making a steady, rhythmic clattering. No lights in the houses, that he could see; everyone away in their beds and fast asleep, if they weren't woken by the racket the carriage was making.

It was a fairly clear night, warm and still, and Daniel could see there were a lot of stars out in the night sky – not like wintertime, when every house burned any number of fires and the fog could get so thick it felt like you could cut it with your knife. Like the knife he'd realized, some time back, that he had in his trouser pocket. Mr. Dooley and Mr. Husker had obviously not searched him very well, if at all, and didn't know he had it. But he wasn't stupid enough to waste this opportunity by using the blade here and now; for now it felt good to know that he had both a weapon and a tool that might come in very handy later.

"Aitch!"

Daniel jumped as Husker leaned forward and rapped on the window.

"What now?"

"Pull up just ahead, where it's darkest."

"What for?"

"We're getting close and I got to bag the boy up again...don't want anyone as knows us to see we had the sack undone. Word could get back."

"Whoa boy..." Dooley reined in the horse and brought the carriage to a halt by a small fenced park. "Always one step ahead, ain'cher, Jake."

"Better'n being caught on the wrong foot." Husker picked up a piece of rope from the floor. "Sit still, boy. And no funny business, mind..."

As Daniel allowed himself to be tied up, gagged and covered by the sack, he thought about being one step ahead. He'd seen something that was going to happen to Dooley, but couldn't see how that knowledge would do him any good. That part he hadn't seen yet.

# CHAPTER 14
# A CAT OUT OF THE BAG

Unable to steady himself with his hands, Daniel leaned into the corner of the brougham, pushing back with his feet as hard as he could so he wouldn't fall over again, should the carriage hit another pothole or take a corner too fast. Now in complete darkness, the musty, coarse sacking still slightly damp to the touch, tied tight above him, Daniel felt trapped like a butterfly in a cocoon.

He could feel the fear, like bile, rise from his stomach.

Soon, too soon for his comfort, he'd be meeting Mr. Carter Bland, who was not going to be very happy to find him instead of Josie Finnister when the sack was opened. How unhappy could mean the difference between living and dying. Daniel felt the most alone and abandoned in his whole life, more so than he ever had, even when thinking about his lot as an orphan. Hannah was forever telling him he was a child who had luck – the luck to be saved as a baby and the luck to be loved. She always hugged him when she said it, and what he would give right now for one of those hugs! That and the knowledge his luck was still with him.

All around he could hear raucous calls from the street, drunken arguments, shrill voices raised in anger, crude laughter. All the sounds of nightlife and fast living. The carriage, which had been moving slower, came to a sudden halt and Daniel could hear Dooley yelling at people to get out of his way, then he heard Husker let his window down and join in the shouting, threatening and cajoling.

Whatever the problem was, it finally sorted itself out and the carriage moved on once more, minutes later turning off into a quieter side street and then coming to a stop. They must, thought Daniel, have arrived at The Ace, wherever that was.

The brougham rocked from side to side and Daniel

heard Dooley grunt as he jumped to the ground, and then let loose a barrage of cussing and swearing; it seemed to be mainly about wanting to throttle whoever had tipped whatever he'd stepped in onto the street.

"Stay with the carriage, Aitch." Daniel realized Husker was getting out and closing the door. "I'm off in to tell Mr. Bland we're arrived; when I give you the whistle, bring her in."

"Her?"

"*Yes!*" A fierce whisper. "*Her*, Aitch...Josie-bleedin-Finnister, what we were sent to fetch, right? Am...I... right?"

"A'course...yes, Jake...I'm with yer."

"I hope so, Dooley, I do hope so..."

Footsteps walked away, then stopped and came back. A finger poked Daniel sharply in the chest.

"No nonsense from you, boy, remember...and Aitch, tie a knot in your tongue when we're in there. For all our sakes."

"Got it, Jake. Dumb as a post." The footsteps disappeared into the distance, followed, much closer, by a deep sigh. "Look at me boots...covered in cack, dammit-to-Hell."

It was hard to know how long the wait was as he'd lost all sense of time, but when Daniel heard a whistle like the call a peewit makes, coming from somewhere quite nearby, he wished it'd been longer. There was an answering whistle from Dooley, then the door to the carriage opened and Daniel was dragged unceremoniously off the seat and flung over Dooley's shoulder.

They went a few yards, and then the sound of the man's footsteps changed, now echoing slightly – they must have left the street... Were they in an alleyway? And then it felt like they were going up some steps. Through the rough weave of the sacking Daniel could see light, hear the hiss of a gas lamp.

"Carry her more delicate, Aitch." Husker's voice, right next to him.

"Eh?"

"More ladylike, carry her more *lady*like."

Daniel felt himself being shifted until he was held, almost like a baby, in Dooley's arms.

"Up the back stairs is it, Jake?"

"Mr. Bland's waiting..."

Hampton Dooley followed his partner down a narrow, badly lit passage; now that he was carrying the boy – *not* the boy...the *girl*! – now that he was carrying *her* in his arms he had to walk sideways, past the entrance to the basement kitchen stairs. The aroma of roasting meats, rising in pungent clouds from below, made his mouth water and stomach rumble as he edged up the creaking, uncarpeted staircase used by the skivvies and servants to get to the other floors. One day...one day he'd like to come into The Ace through the front entrance, where butlers and flunkeys welcomed the bigwigs, come to play at the gaming tables.

But that was unlikely to happen very soon, as this job was turning out to be a lot more taxing than he'd imagined when Jake had first told him about it. He had to admit that he preferred it when all he was asked to do was top someone, the dead being a lot less problematic than the living, in his humble opinion.

He had no idea what Carter Bland's reaction was going to be when the sack was opened, but he was glad Jake would be the one doing the talking; he'd heard many a story about Mr. Bland's temper and none of them good. Still and all, the money was tasty and Hampton Dooley could take any amount of verbal if there was decent money at the end of it. Though it did occur to him, as Jake reached the door at the top of the stairs, went through and held it open, that delivering the wrong person wasn't the best way to guarantee getting paid.

"He's not going to settle us tonight, is he Jake?"

"Shut it!"

"He's not, is he?" Dooley whispered.

Husker shrugged. "Unlikely, considering."

"Not even something?"

"Maybe..."

"Think we might get a bit to kill the little runt?"

Silence.

Jacob Husker looked at his partner, one eyebrow raised, lips a thin, pale sneer. He didn't say a word (he didn't need to), just raised his right hand and drew a finger slowly across his mouth; head to one side he raised both eyebrows in an unspoken question: did Dooley understand? Dooley nodded that he did.

Husker turned on his heels and walked down the panelled, gaslit corridor, along a wide strip of thick, burgundy red carpet, stopping in front of a door with a large, polished brass handle. He looked back at Dooley, beckoning him to follow, then rapped on the door and waited. A muffled voice barked a reply. Taking a deep breath, Husker reached for the handle, pausing for a moment before he twisted it, then pushed the door open and walked into the room.

Dooley went in after him and found himself being ushered through into a second room, and a very fine place it was. Just the smells alone were exotic, expensive and redolent of money, class and style: a heady, delicate mix of fine tobaccos, beeswax polish, leather, brandy, wine and perfume filled a large, high-ceilinged room where brass, crystal and silver glowed. Everywhere he looked oak, walnut and mahogany shone and everything seemed hushed, luxurious, perfect.

Behind a massive leather-covered desk, his chair turned so that he was looking out of the tall window into the night, sat a man, his black hair shiny with pomade and sporting what looked to be a fine set of mutton-chop whiskers.

"Close the door, Mr. Husker. Can't do business with the world listening in." His voice sounded as oiled as his hair, and while Husker did as he'd been asked, Carter Bland turned round in his chair, looked at Dooley and made a face like he'd smelled something bad. "What in the name of Heaven and Hell have you brought her here in?"

"A sack, Mr. Bland."

"Purloined, no doubt, from some farmer's sewer of a ditch..." Bland took a large white handkerchief out and waved it in front of his pale, slightly pudgy face. "Get her out of it and get *it* out of *here*!"

"Right away, sir." Husker nodded at his partner, indicating that Dooley should put the sack down. "Let her stand, Aitch."

Dooley nodded; tight-lipped he bent down and

gently placed "Josie" upright on the floor, facing Carter Bland, holding the sack-covered figure steady. Husker came over and moved him out of the way, standing behind the figure.

Carter Bland made a business of lighting a pipe, puffing aromatic smoke in a protective screen in front of him. "Get on with it, man!"

Husker, in the manner of a showman, took a steel clasp knife out of his pocket, flicked out a blade with his thumbnail and sliced through the rope holding the sack closed using a single upward cut. With a flourish he pulled the sack down and performed a very low bow, which meant he was looking at the floor and not the person who'd been in the sack. "Miss Josie Finnister, Mr. Bland...as requested."

Thankfully the look of astonishment registered by Dooley was quite genuine (he'd never seen Husker put on such a performance before), but it was nothing when compared to the total incredulity etched on Carter Bland's face. Eyes wide, mouth agape, and pointing across his desk, he was speechless, mainly because he was choking, having inhaled far too much pipe smoke.

In mock concern, Husker rushed across to him. "A tot of brandy, Mr. Bland? Shall I call down for some water maybe?"

Bland hacked a couple of times, wiping his mouth

with his handkerchief and stood, pushing his chair back so fast it almost toppled over. "Who…? What…?"

"Are you quite all right, sir?"

"Am I quite…?" Bland looked at Husker as if he'd gone mad. "Just who in the name of Beelzebub's *arse* is that?"

Dooley watched Husker turn to look, as if for the first time, at who was standing there, bound and gagged, with the sack around his ankles. He looked and looked again, rushed halfway across the carpeted floor and stopped, his face a picture of complete amazement. "I…I don't understand…"

"*You* don't understand, Mr. Husker? That, if I might say, is the least of it!" Bland thumped the desk with his fist. "Who is this…this *peasant*? Where is the person I *asked* you to bring me?"

"Mr. Bland…" Husker, the picture of a dumbfounded man, stood slack-jawed and shaking his head. "We found her, right where we were told she'd be, at this circus…staked the place out, went back, dead of night, to her caravan and took her…sweet, no trouble at all."

"So who the hellfire do we have here, then?" Bland moved round the desk, frowning and peering at the small figure in front of him. "And it's a *boy*, dammit – are you blind as well as stupid, can't you tell the difference?"

*"So who the hellfire do we have here, then?"*

"It was black as pitch, Mr. Bland, just the one person in there, right Aitch?" Dooley nodded, but Bland wasn't looking at him, just staring at the grimy, crumpled boy in front of him. "Honest to God, Mr. Bland, there was nowhere else she should've been, and we never opened the sack till just now!"

Dooley had to admit, it was a masterful performance.

Bland looked Daniel up and down, then around the room. "Where's the bag? I said to bring her bag – did you look for any papers, man?"

Dooley glanced at Husker. He wondered if his partner had forgotten all about the bag as well.

"As I say, Mr. Bland, we were like blind men in that caravan. I tried, but before I could find it, we heard people in the vicinity and took what we could without getting caught."

"Your incompetence is astounding, sir! Astounding! You there." Bland pointed at Dooley. "Take the gag off..." Waiting until Dooley had untied the frayed piece of cloth, he then leaned forward. "What's your name, boy?"

"Daniel."

"Well, Daniel, are you any the wiser than these two buffoons as to why *you* are standing here and not a lady of my acquaintance called Miss Josie Finnister?" Daniel shook his head; slowly Bland turned to look at Husker, a humourless smile on his face. "Did she pay you to do this?"

"On my life, Mr. Bland, I never spoke to the lady, just watched and waited and went back when the time was right. May I be struck down, but this ain't nothing to do with me."

"Oh, but it's *everything* to do with you, Mr. Husker, everything. It's business, very important business, so get rid of this urchin, go back to wherever you've just come from and *bring me Josie Finnister*! I want that woman, not some snivelling wretch of a boy." Bland walked back behind his desk, pulled up his chair and sat down. "Do I make myself quite, quite clear?"

Husker nodded. "Let the boy go and—"

"Get *rid* of the boy, I said get *rid* of him. No trace."

"But..."

"But what? Are you questioning my orders?" Bland raised an inquiring eyebrow. "If you want *any* money at all, Mr. Husker, you'd do well to go, now."

"I was just thinking, Mr. Bland, that someone might want him back."

"Him?" Bland's nose wrinkled. "In Heaven's name why?"

"He's somebody's child."

"Are you implying that, as you found him in Miss Finnister's caravan he might be something to do with her? How completely improbable!" Bland glanced at Daniel. "Are you Josie's secret child, boy?"

"No, sir."

"No, sir, didn't think so. But then, on the other hand..." Bland picked up his pipe and lit it again, silent and pensive for a long, long moment. "As you say, Husker, he is *someone's* son...you belong to somebody, don't you, boy – who's that then?"

"James Hubble, sir."

Husker nodded. "That was the name of the circus, Mr. Bland...Hubble's Circus, that was the name."

"Well, well, all is not completely lost, Mr. Husker... I do believe we quite possibly have an item here with which we may bargain. I do really." Carter Bland sat back in his chair, tapping his teeth with the stem of the pipe. "Though I have to say I am not, as you might imagine, best pleased with your work thus far. I have come to expect better, so much better from you. I had such confidence...anyway, Mr. Husker, now you have the chance to redeem yourself."

"My pleasure to do so, Mr. Bland."

"I've no doubt."

"What would you like me to do?"

"Get this boy out of here and take him over to The Sun, put him down in the cellars under lock and key. Your silent friend," Bland nodded at Dooley, "can act as guard and watchman. Then you come back here forthwith, if not sooner. Understood?"

Husker felt as if Bland was expecting him to pull his forelock and back out of the room like an indentured servant. Instead, he bowed slightly. "On winged feet, Mr. Bland."

"Are you *mocking* me, Mr. Husker?" Carter Bland's eyes narrowed, becoming almost hooded, and his cheeks reddened. An icy silence cut the room.

"No, sir."

"Just as well," Bland turned his back on them. "I wouldn't like that at all..."

## CHAPTER 15

# UNDERNEATH THE SUN

Daniel didn't know what he felt – certainly relief at still being alive and not "got rid of", like it seemed was going to happen before Mr. Carter Bland changed his mind. But also, standing in the room in The Ace, he knew that he was an insignificant pawn in some game where he didn't know the rules and had no idea what was happening. And that made him feel angry.

From the moment Husker had opened the sack Daniel had been treated as if he was no better than some animal, valuable only because he belonged to someone. Waiting in that room, hemmed in by all the magnificence that money could buy, observing the person it all belonged to (an evil man, who Daniel felt sure didn't deserve the beautiful objects he surrounded himself with), Daniel had realized the place was just about showing how rich and powerful he was. Everything there only because it was expensive.

In an odd way he hadn't been connected to events unfolding in the room, so he was able to watch, almost from a distance, what was going on. To his way of thinking Mr. Carter Bland, for all his wealth and manners and education, was a snake of a man, low, lethal and cowardly. Daniel knew what honesty looked like...it had a battered, some would say ugly face, scarred knuckles and a rough way of talking. He hoped he'd be there if ever Mr. Hubble met Mr. Bland.

He remembered the question Carter Bland had put to him – *Who do you belong to?* – and his immediate answer – *Mr. Hubble* – because that was the truth, that's whose name he had. But his family...who did he *really* belong to? He could have come from anywhere, have belonged to anyone, but he thought of his family as Billy and Hannah, first and foremost, and then Mr. Hubble. But he didn't feel as if he *belonged* to any one of them.

Maybe that was because it was the circus he truly belonged to.

He'd never been away from those people for even a day in his whole life and he missed them all so much. So much that it made his throat hurt and he knew tears could come very easily. But he would never let that happen. Never let these people see him do that.

He'd stood stock-still while they'd talked about him as if he wasn't there, and he'd let himself be bundled up in the sack again and slung over Dooley's shoulder (no ladylike treatment this time). Once out of earshot of their employer, Dooley had started to complain about how hungry and tired he was, Husker reminding him curtly that he wasn't the one who was going to have to turn about and come straight back to The Ace.

"Why'd you have to come to The Sun with me – don't he trust me to do the job, then?" Dooley shrugged Daniel off his shoulder and onto the brougham's floor as if he was a sack of vegetables and stomped off to climb up onto the driver's seat.

"He don't trust either of us, at this moment."

"What am I s'posed to do with him, Jake?"

"Feed and water him, and make sure the little blighter don't get away."

"Jake?"

"What?"

"You never looked for that bag, did you."

"I did. Momentarily." Husker shook his head. "There was no time, Aitch...it was as dark as a black dog's hide in there and too many people all around; we'd a got caught if we'd stayed any longer."

"Reckon so."

"And that girl might've been stupid enough to take something from Mr. Bland, Aitch, but I don't think she'd've took it with her when she ran." Husker put a foot up on the brougham's step. "I reckon it's hid, maybe even in the alehouse. You never know, we might even find it before we have to go and fetch the girl. If we look hard enough..."

The place Daniel was in, down in the cellars of The Sun, was a dank, fetid space with no candle, no furniture and he could hear the skittering of small creatures. As Dooley had pushed him in, Daniel had realized, in the flickering light of the oil lamp the man was holding, that it was the room he'd seen, in that weird way he did, on the journey up to London.

Sitting on a straw palliasse in a small alcove set into one of the walls, chewing on a piece of what tasted like day-old bread, he replayed the scene again and again and the only conclusion he could come to was that, somehow, he would get out of this place. But how?

He was tired and hungry, but determined, before he fell asleep, to try and think of something.

They might have untied him, but he was locked up, he was underground and he was in complete darkness. The morning was going to have to come before any light at all made it through the tiny barred window set high in the locked door, before he would be able to see exactly what his chances for escape were. Precious few, he had little doubt. As he lay down on the thin mattress he wondered if anyone else had been locked up in here before him, and if they'd ever lived to tell the tale…

Even though the day had been a long one, Josie couldn't sleep. They'd had to wait some time for a train, and once they were aboard the journey had been hours of dust and tedium, with Hubble uncharacteristically jumpy and nervous due to it being his first time journeying by steam. Sam Baston had just sat, impassive and unmoved by everything going on around him, leaving Josie to her thoughts.

On arrival at Paddington Station – a vast cathedral of steel and glass, chaos, smoke and a whole congregation of people – they'd made their way outside to the rank where the cabs waited for passengers. Josie was wearing a hat with a veil, the better to remain anonymous, with Hubble, somewhat quieter and paler than normal after his journey, on her left and Sam on her right. She'd known they made a spectacle from the way they were looked at by all and sundry. She knew people were wondering, *Who could she be, this mysterious black-veiled woman with this pair of mismatched companions?* She would, she had no doubts, be the subject of a good few conversations.

From Paddington they'd made their way through town, along Oxford Street, across Regent's Street and past the rookeries of St Giles – from shops selling the best the world could bring to London, to a place where she knew the filthy streets were so narrow they made alleyways look like avenues. Turning down Charing Cross Road they'd gone on into Seven Dials, the cabbie complaining that he'd be lucky to pick up a decent fare in those streets.

Josie knew Seven Dials was no place for an honest person, and had said so; Bruise had readily agreed, but countered with the fact that few, if anyone, would come looking for them there either. And he said he knew good people and safe places in Seven Dials. And don't believe everything the face of a house tells you, he'd added, as they drew up outside a particularly dilapidated building.

* * *

Josie stood at the window of her room, staring out across the sagging, higgledy-piggledy rooftops of a moonlit Seven Dials and watched the night sky start to fray and turn the palest, palest salmon pink at its eastern edge. From the outside it was hard to believe that, behind the weathered, careworn exterior and shabbily curtained ground-floor windows, behind a front door that looked like it had last seen paint a hundred years before, there were rooms she was sure were like those she imagined were in the finest hotels. Bruise's safe house was a wonder.

Turning her back on the window, she wondered where Daniel could be, and whether he was still alive, now that Carter Bland must have found out his plan had gone so badly awry. No matter what Bruise said, she couldn't blame Hannah, or anyone else in the circus for that matter, for thinking Daniel's disappearance was her fault. It most certainly *was* her fault. If she hadn't gone to the circus, he would still be there. And however hard she tried she couldn't stop thinking about the look of accusation on Hannah's face. She knew herself the pain of losing someone you loved.

Josie also knew that in this life, if you waited to be given something you would, as a rule, get nothing. That's why, when Opportunity had tapped her on the shoulder, she'd taken the papers from Carter Bland's office; fortune rarely repeated itself. And now that Chance had turned on her, slippery as an eel, she had to keep her wits about her and help in every way to get the boy back. For Bruise's sake, if nothing else.

For now, though, she needed rest. Josie yawned, blinked eyes that were now gritty with tiredness and turned away from the window and the approaching dawn...

It had either been early morning noises from the streets up above, or, more likely, something large scurrying over him that had woken Daniel from his shallow, disturbed sleep. In what little dawn light seeped into the room he watched a large brown rat jump off the mattress to the floor and disappear into the shadows; sitting up, wondering what else he was sharing this bed with, he looked round his prison.

Not much to see: damp, mouldering brickwork; a curved, half-barrel brick ceiling; a solid, iron-studded wooden door with no handle on the inside, and that, apart from the mattress in the tiny alcove, looked like it was everything. Daniel got up and stood in the middle of the ten foot wide by twelve, maybe fourteen foot long room, turning slowly round, examining the place from floor to ceiling for anything that might give him an idea how he could get out.

Nothing.

Then he began a closer, more detailed search, just in case there was *something* (a tunnel? Well, you never knew) hidden in the deeper shadows. Again, nothing. Except he did find a loose brick, which he eventually managed, with the help of his knife, to get out; Daniel looked at the brick in his hands, for a moment considering the possibility of starting his own tunnel...but then again, probably not. He closed his knife, put it back in his pocket and sat back down on the palliasse, the straw it was filled with almost compressed into a solid block; he stared in front of him, letting his mind wander in search of a scheme.

He had no idea how much time he'd spent just thinking, or what time of day it was. He had a feeling it might be still quite early as there'd been no noises that he could hear coming from inside the tavern, and only the occasional sound of a cart passing by in the street. No one had come down to check on him or give him anything to eat and drink, and after all his pondering there'd been one simple conclusion he'd been able to come to – the only way he was going to get out was the way he'd got in. Somehow he *had* to get past whoever next opened the door.

It was more than likely going to be Dooley, who was

big and strong but no quick wit. But what could he do? Try and rush past him? It was a thought, but one more likely to get him a cuffed ear than anything else, Dooley being about as wide as the doorway.

Daniel glanced back at the door. It wasn't rectangular, but had a semicircular top with a sort of curved ledge of bricks sticking out that continued to run all the way round the four walls. Head on one side, he measured the gap between the narrow brick ledge and the vaulted ceiling, calculating, seeing if the tiny seed of an idea he'd had could actually take root. He got up and walked over to the door, not looking at it but instead examining the state of the wall. There was a chance. A small one, but still, a chance.

He went back to the alcove, sat down and took his shoes off, tying the laces together and hanging the shoes around his neck. Walking back to the door, he reached up with his right arm and grabbed at the narrow space between the bricks where the ancient mortar had started to turn to dust and by doing so had created space for his fingertips to get some purchase. He lifted his left leg and searched for a similar space with his toes, found some and then pulled himself up, starting to climb the wall like a spider.

Almost up to where he could get a firmer stance by using the window as a step, Daniel heard a door being opened; leaning round so he could peer through the bars, he saw a harsh shard of light had been cast on the cellar wall, motes of dust dancing a jig in it. And then he heard someone coming down the creaking wooden staircase. Assuming it was Dooley, Daniel dropped lightly to the floor and ran back to the alcove, heart pounding, cursing under his breath that he might never have the chance to see if his plan would work.

As he bit his lip, waiting for the cell door to be unlocked, he heard a muffled voice yell out and the footsteps stopped. A young girl's voice screeched back, "Eh? What yer say?" in reply and then Daniel heard a loud sigh, footsteps on the stairs again and the door shutting with a loud slam.

The silence was broken by a small black mouse scurrying from one side of the room to the other. Daniel shook his head and let out the breath he'd been holding. It seemed like he'd better get a move on as at least some of the tavern's residents were finally up and greeting the day.

Now he knew where the finger- and toe-holds were he was back up the wall in no time and, with his right foot lodged against one of the window bars he was ready to go. He tensed and then launched himself upwards, toes searching for the ledge, hands reaching for the ceiling...and he so nearly made it. So, so nearly.

Landing back down on the stone flagging, a jolt running through his bones, he stood straight up and went back to the wall.

In the end it took him three more tries before he managed to land with both feet on the narrow ledge, his arms shooting upwards as if spring-loaded. And then, there he was, standing above the door facing the wall. Only one more move to make. The crucial one. Get this wrong and he'd be in trouble.

He knew full well that what he was doing broke every one of Billy's rules, but he didn't have time for hours of practice to iron out all the risks. This had to work first time, because he was getting tired and if he fell from this height onto stone flagging he might well hurt himself quite badly. Taking a deep breath Daniel began moving, inching his hands together until they crossed, right over left. Twisting himself in a tight corkscrew movement, he pivoted on his right foot...and a split second later he was facing the room. His back was now almost glued to the brickwork, his feet together and arms up and out to the sides, palms pressed against the curved ceiling.

All he had to do was stay there until someone came into the room.

## CHAPTER 16

# THE LITTLE DUKE

To keep his mind off the hunger pangs gnawing at his stomach and the cramping pains in his arms and legs, Daniel tried to occupy himself with running over the next stage of his plan, but his thoughts kept on returning to the circus. He wondered what was happening there... Were they on the move to a new site? What would Mr. Hubble be doing? He knew Hannah wouldn't let him rest until he'd done something about trying to find him, of that he was absolutely sure. And what of Comus and Seth and Jem and everyone else?

They were out there, doing the things they always did, and here he was, kept like a common thief in this cell of a room in the tavern Josie used to run. All Daniel wanted with all his heart was to be back out in the open, in the fresh air and with his friends, but he knew he mustn't let this desperation and longing push him into making a stupid mistake. If he had any chance at all of getting out of this place, it was a very slim one indeed.

And then, with such clarity he could almost smell him, Daniel remembered Savage and could hardly bear the thought that he might not ever see him again, might never ride him, free like the wind, on his own through open meadows or into the ring to the cheers of a town or village crowd. Such black thoughts brought him back to the present, taut, aching muscles and all, and made him all the more determined that he *had* to make his plan work.

Some time later – it seemed like an age – the door to the cellar opened again, someone coughed loudly and hacked like a sick mule, and then Daniel heard footsteps, this time heavier than before. Someone in boots dragging their feet down the stairs. Someone, he wondered, who might have had a drink or two last night and just have woken up?

Boots clumped across the stone floor towards the door above which he was standing and, like the moments before entering the ring, Daniel's mind focused entirely on what he was going to be doing in the next few seconds and minutes. But entirely unlike a performance, which he would have practised under Billy's eagle eye, over and over, this show would happen only once.

The footsteps stopped outside the door, it sounded like something was being put down on the floor and Daniel heard the metallic jingle of keys. Then came a confused grunt and mumbled curses, followed by a scrabbling sound he believed must be someone trying frantically to get a key into a keyhole.

Exactly as he'd hoped, whoever was outside the room must have peered through the little barred window and seen that it looked like the occupant might have somehow managed to escape. A louder string of curses was followed by the key finally going home and being turned, and then the door was wrenched open.

"Boy!" It was Dooley, his head stuck forward and turning side to side like a chicken after corn. "Where the..."

Looking down, Daniel willed Dooley to take at least one, no more than two steps further into the room. He did. And as soon as he had, Daniel bent his legs and leaped off the ledge in a move he'd run over in his head so many times it was almost like he'd done it before; curling over into a tight ball he brought his knees up, completing a somersault in mid-air and then jabbing his legs down, like they were pistons. His timing wasn't quite perfect, but it was good enough; his heels met Dooley's thick neck like a hammer meets the head of a nail and the man keeled over, falling straight to the floor as if he was a tree that had been chopped down.

Daniel, who'd fallen backwards and rolled onto the floor, picked himself up, shook his head and looked down at Dooley, twitching and groaning on the dirty flagstones. He kneeled down by him. "Say goodbye to Mr. Husker when you see him..." he whispered, then ran out of the room faster than if demons and devils were after him.

He had no idea how long Dooley might remain stunned and he had to get the room locked as fast as possible. Putting his shoulder to it, he pushed the door to, reached up and turned the key, putting it, along with the two or three others on the same ring, in his jerkin pocket. Only then did he give himself a moment to stretch his aching body.

Sitting down on the cold floor, about to put his shoes back on, he saw a battered metal tray with a small jug of ale and piece of bread on it. He grabbed the bread and as he devoured it, dipped in the beer to soften it, he tied his laces and listened for any movements and sounds which might give him clues as to what was going on in the rest of the tavern – or whether Dooley was coming to.

He might well be out of the room, but Daniel now had to get out of the building itself without being seen or caught. Houses and buildings generally were mysteries to him; he had no notion of how they worked. In the world of the circus there were no cellars or second storeys. But he imagined there would be quite a few people living in the tavern as well as Dooley and probably Husker, if he'd come back from his meeting with Mr. Bland the night before. A lot of people to avoid.

Daniel stood up, stretching again, feeling the blood flow back into the tips of his fingers. He could hear Dooley moving on the other side of the locked door, and he couldn't risk staying a moment longer in this place as the man might start yelling fit to wake the dead at any moment, bringing everyone down to the cellar. Looking round, he realized that, once again, he was faced with the fact that he was somewhere with only one exit. It was the stairs or nothing.

Taking a final swig of musty ale, Daniel went over to the stairs and listened...he could hear voices, but he wasn't sure where they were coming from. There were no choices here, he was going to have to make a dash for it. With one last glance towards the locked room in which he'd been kept, he ran lightly up the stairs to the half-open door at the top and stopped. No sounds, no voices, no one anywhere near.

Slipping out of the cellar and quietly shutting the door, he found himself in a narrow passage with three other doors going off it. But which one to take? He stared at each in turn, hoping one would give him some kind of feeling it was the door to choose...and then he knew. All three of the doors had small, square panes of glass set into them, but the door to his right was the one with the brightest light coming through it, meaning it must, surely, lead outside rather than inside. Surely.

As he walked over to it and was about to reach for the latch, Daniel heard one of the doors behind him open and he froze.

"An' who might you be?" It was a girl's voice, and sounded like the one he'd heard before.

Daniel turned to look. She was young, maybe his age, hard to tell, and was looking questioningly at him; he didn't want to hurt this girl, but he wasn't going to let her do anything that would get him caught. "I'm in the wrong place..."

"That so?"

Daniel nodded.

"Well, better not be here, then, I'd say."

"What?"

"Better go, an't you."

"S'pose I'd better..." Daniel turned to go.

"You're the one they brought in here late, aren'cha? Stuck you in the cellars, din't he, that big bloke what works for Mr. Bland...I *'ate* that Mr. Bland, I do." The girl's lip curled. "Where is that Dooley, then?"

Daniel shook his head. "No idea."

The girl smiled. "Bet you do..." She nodded to herself. "*He's* a pig, too."

"Is he?"

"That's a fact." The girl smiled at him. "The yard's empty right now, but be quick about it."

He was out and away, but, for some strange reason Daniel still felt twitchy and nervous. As if every step he took was being watched. As the girl had promised, the tavern's yard was empty and he'd been able to slip out through the gates and into the street like a draught. He'd wanted to run, to put as much distance between himself and The Sun as he could, and in as short a time as possible. Except he realized behaviour like that might just draw the wrong kind of attention, so he walked, in as jaunty a way as he could, until he was far enough away to be able to relax slightly.

Once he stopped worrying so much, Daniel realized he was lost, having blindly taken this turning and then that, until he was so confused he thought he might be adrift for ever in this vast, sprawling city, choked with people and animals, carriages and carts. On his own, with no money, no food and no friends. This depressing thought made him stop and look for somewhere to sit and think about what he should do next.

The street he was in was a reasonably busy thoroughfare, lined in almost equal parts with shops, businesses and houses. A working part of the city; not grand, but no slum either. A few yards down the street he saw there was a church, with steps leading up to its columned entrance. Daniel could see no reason why anyone would begrudge him resting there on this sunny summer morning. As he sat down on the warm stone, though, the unnerving feeling came back that he was being observed, studied, scrutinized. And then across the street, standing by a lamp post and eating an apple, he saw someone watching him. Smiling.

It was a boy, maybe two, three years older than him from his face, but appearing small for his age. Dressed in clothes that were just a bit too big, and which had definitely seen better days, he wore a slightly battered peaked cap and a wide grin. And now he was walking across the street towards him. When he was a couple of feet away, the boy threw an apple at Daniel, who caught it easily with one hand.

"Have you been following me?" Daniel stood up, ready, if necessary, to do whatever it took to get away, and found he was an inch or so taller than the boy.

"Might 'ave...and then again, might not." The boy took a large bite out of his apple, juice running down his chin, and stood there chewing, looking up from underneath the peak of his old cap.

"Who are you anyway?"

"Tom," came the reply through a mouthful of apple. "Tom Ducato. You?"

Daniel's stomach rumbled so loud the boy, Tom, heard it and laughed. Daniel held up his apple. "This for me?"

Tom nodded, looking up and down the street. "They call me Little Duke."

Daniel took a bite. "Who do?"

"People what know me."

Daniel smiled, it felt like for the first time in days. "They call *me* Crown Prince Juan Pablo of Nicobar."

Tom's face jerked round, a look of puzzled surprise pasted on it. "They do, do they? Why's that then, you royal or sunnink?"

"Not likely, I ride in a circus...Mr. Hubble, the man who owns it, it's the name he gave me for the show."

"So what's yer proper moniker?"

"Daniel Hubble."

"It's your pa what runs the place then?"

"Sort of..."

"Well 'tis, or 'tisn't, Mr. Crown Prince...can't be both."

"I'm an..." Daniel stopped, wondering why he was telling this boy about himself.

"You're a what?"

Daniel shrugged; what harm could it do? "I'm an orphan...Mr. Hubble gave me his name."

"Often wish someone had adopted me...might've got me rightful place, leading the life of Riley with a toff for me pa, stead of the geezer I got. Only thing *he* ever gived me was a good slapping. So what's it like, being a prince?"

"I'm not a prince, I told you, it's just a name." Daniel threw his apple core into the gutter and looked the boy up and down; it occurred to him that this boy might believe he really was some kind of prince. "Why did you start following me anyway?"

"Get Lord Muck – I'm just trying to be a friendly fellow!"

"You don't know me, why d'you want to be my friend? You think I'm some straw-sucker just up from the country or something?"

"Well beggin' yer lordship's pardon, sir." Tom doffed his cap. "'Scuse *me* for being a Good Samaritan to a lad what's as lost as the Battle of Trafalgar, if you was a Frenchman, or a Spaniard come to that."

Daniel couldn't work this boy out, his edgy friendliness made him wary. Living in a circus all his life, he'd come across just about every kind of person – good coves, the very worst ones and everything in-between. He believed, like Mr. Hubble said, that no stranger ever did you a favour without wanting some small thing in return, that there was always a side to everyone's story. But for the life of him he couldn't work out what this Tom Ducato was up to – could he *really* think he was some kind of prince? If he did, then he had straw for brains, but if he *was* prepared to help, Daniel would take up the offer, as far as it went, and see where it got him. He'd just keep his eyes polished.

"Look..." Daniel picked a bit of apple skin out from between his teeth, then glanced at Tom.

"What?"

Daniel considered his next move; the only plan he had was that he should get back to The Ace because it was the one place he could think of where Mr. Hubble, when he came looking for him, which he surely must do, would go to. And he needed someone to help him get there. Someone like Tom Ducato, maybe...

"There's a place I have to get to...but I got no money or nothing to pay you with, if you help me get there, until I meet up with my people."

Tom attempted to look put out, but made too much of it. "You think all I'm after is gelt?" Daniel didn't say a word. "So, Danny-boy...'ow much will I get?"

"I'm sure Mr. Hubble will make it worth your while, when we find him."

"If he's in this town, then I can find him!" Tom put out his hand. "A duke should at all times help a prince, I always says! Follow me..."

"But you don't know where I want to go!"

"All in good time, all in good time yer lordship..."

# CHAPTER 17

# DO AS YOU WOULD BE DONE BY

With an arm round Daniel's shoulder and refusing to take no for an answer, Tom Ducato led the way through a maze of side streets, ducking into alleyways and crossing teeming courtyards until he finally stopped outside a tenement building exactly like a hundred others they'd gone past.

"Here we are!"

Daniel shook his head. "Where?"

"It's me place...leastways, where I come back to most often."

"What are we doing here?"

"Why, we've come to visit me dear old ma, wot always has something tasty ready for the eating." Tom pushed open the front door. "'Cos me, I can't help anyone on an empty stomach, never could."

Leading the way up a flight of bare wooden stairs and along a gloomy landing, the walls of which had lost most of their plaster and showed great expanses of laths, Tom stopped outside the only door and knocked. Daniel looked at him, thinking it was an odd thing to do in your own home, but then thought maybe it was the kind of thing people did when they lived in houses. Mr. Hubble, who had once lived in houses, liked people to knock.

"Someone there?" The voice, screechy as an unoiled wheel, came from right behind the door.

"Me – Little Duke, Ma!" Tom winked at Daniel. "On my word, she's a veritable treasure."

The door opened a crack, a tiny, wizened face appearing, one milky eye squinting up at them. "Who's this?"

"A friend in need, Ma."

"Do we like him?"

"Oh that we do, Ma."

"Better bring the lad in then." A small age-spotted

hand, gold rings on every bony finger, some of them glinting with what looked like diamonds, gripped the door and pulled it open. "Any friend of Little Duke's is a friend of Old Meggy's...come in, come in!"

Tom ushered Daniel into the room, a large, high-ceilinged space, but so crammed with furniture and boxes piled on boxes and with a selection of threadbare Persian rugs covering every inch of the floor, that it was actually quite cramped. It was also stuffily hot, the windows shut tight with heavy, dark-blue drapes half pulled across them as if it was winter and not a sunny August morning; there was a fire burning in the small range, and the cloying aroma of lily of the valley almost, but not quite, masked the various smells of communal living and inefficient plumbing.

"Anything to eat, Ma?"

"Always got something, aven' I?" The old lady's face crinkled up so much as she smiled that her eyes disappeared. "That's why you lot loves me so much – in't that right?"

"True enough, Ma – shall we sit down?"

"Move the cats an' I'll bring over a couple of nice bowls a stew 'n' dumplins for the two of you."

Tom threaded his way over to a table and swept a couple of mangy cats off onto the floor, where they sat and hissed at him. "Sit down, Danny-boy, make yerself at home."

"What's 'is name? Did you say?" Tom's mother, dressed all in black with a small lace cap on top of a mound of wispy grey hair, turned from what she was doing and peered over her shoulder at Daniel.

"He's a prince, Ma – Prince Juan Pablo of somewhere or other!"

"Don't look anything like no prince to me." She turned back to the range. "Someone what's got younger legs had better come an' get these bowls."

Daniel ate the food only because he was ravenously hungry and he didn't want to appear ungrateful. It smelled worse than what the circus dogs ate and it looked like nothing he'd ever seen on a plate before; the stew, a brown paste, with darker brown bits in it, clung like snot to waxy grey lumps he supposed were the dumplings, and everything tasted burned and old. If Tom felt the same way, he didn't show it one bit, instead, watched by his tiny, smiling mother, he cleaned his plate with his fingers and belched loudly as a finale.

"Delicate, Ma, delicate!"

"More, dear?"

"Save me some for later." Tom got up, picking an old

news-sheet off the chair next to him. "I'm off out to the jakes, won't be long!"

Watching him leave the room, Daniel became aware that Tom's mother was staring at him. "Nice cuppa tea, dear? I got a fresh pot keeping hot."

"Please." Daniel nodded.

"What a nice, polite child..." The old lady got up and busied herself at the range again, coming back to the table with a surprisingly delicate china cup filled to the brim with rust-brown liquid, but no saucer. "Drink up, dear."

Daniel took a mouthful of lukewarm, bitter tea. "Has Tom got brothers and sisters?"

"'Ow should I know?"

"But I thought...Tom said you were..."

"What did the little bleeder say about me?"

"That you were his mother."

"Heaven forbid! Gracious me, no – you must've misunderstood!" The old lady cackled at the thought, dabbing a handkerchief at her eyes and nodding her head at Daniel. "His mother! What a thing..."

"But he called you Ma, you must've heard him?"

"I'm just deaf Old Meggy, what can't see very well neither...just someone people bring nice things to, what others come and collect. For money a'course. Sweet boy, that Little Duke, one of me best."

"Best what?"

"Whatever he puts his mind to, but he's got the lightest fingers...never been caught yet, y'know."

"Why did he bring me here?"

"'Ow should I know? But he must've had his reasons, dear...now finish yer cup and get on yer way, will you?"

Daniel looked over at the door. "Tom's gone, hasn't he?"

"'Ow should I know?"

Finishing the last of his tea, Daniel stood up to go. "What's it called, round here, d'you know that at least?"

Ignoring Daniel's sarcasm, Old Meg leaned forward and picked the cup off the table. "This is Clerkenwell, dear, lovely part of town that them stinkin' rozzers and their law don't hardly come to at all." Holding a dusty, fly-specked pair of lorgnette spectacles up to her eyes she squinted at the bottom of the cup. Daniel turned to go. "Don't you want to know, boy?"

"Know what?"

"Yer future, a'course, in the tea leaves."

Daniel walked over to the door. "I can already see it for myself."

Old Meg frowned as she watched the door close behind Daniel. There was something odd about that boy, she'd felt it the moment he'd walked in. She then looked back at the cup in her hand even more closely,

*There was something odd about that boy.*

squinting through her glasses at the tea leaves in the bottom. "*Definitely* a queen...though can't fer the life of me think what a little toe-ragger like that's doing going to see Her Majesty..."

Josie woke up slowly; the insistent knocking that, in her dream, had been something like a woodpecker, was now someone at her door. She yawned and through half-open eyes realized that sunlight was streaming into her room as she hadn't pulled the curtains before eventually going to bed.

"Who is it?"

"The maid, miss...very sorry to disturb you, miss, but Mr. Hubble says could you attend him and Mr. Baston downstairs, miss."

Josie sat up. "What time of day is it?"

"Ten of the clock, miss, or thereabouts...I've got hot water, miss."

"You'd better come in..."

Tom Ducato stood in the shadows of an alleyway, taking a pinch or two of snuff and watching the comings and goings in and out of The Sun tavern. As he watched he reflected on Fate and what a capricious, fickle mistress she was; there he'd been, on his way back to Old Meggy after a pretty poor night's business, when he'd spotted the boy, Daniel. The moment he'd seen him, slinking out of the backyard in the early morning he'd suspected he was a sneak who'd maybe been disturbed while trying to rob the place.

Following the lad as he got himself lost, Tom began to have his doubts; by rights, if he was a thief, he should've made directly for his fence with whatever he'd managed to lift, or to make his excuses if he'd got nothing. When Tom had got up close, by the church, there was something about the boy that didn't fit the picture – not that he believed the story about the circus either – but if the boy was a dipper he wasn't a very good one.

He'd had nothing on him in any of his pockets, apart from a knife on a lanyard which had to stay where it was. Except...Tom pulled the ring of keys he'd lifted out of Daniel's jerkin and examined them, wondering what they opened, imagining what he'd be able to take back to Old Meg's. He smiled to himself, remembering the way she'd played along with him pretending she was his mother; he wasn't all that sure why he'd taken the boy back there as he could just as well have lifted what he wanted off him in the street and been gone before he knew it.

Recalling how it'd been for him when he'd first started, he thought maybe he'd felt sorry for him, this dirty, hungry, black-haired wastrel. He'd have to watch that...in his position it didn't do to start thinking like that about people. If it got out, talk might go round he was getting soft.

He looked back at the tavern, instantly forgetting about Daniel and concentrating on working out how he'd get in the place when he came back much, much later.

Josie, feeling quite the lady after the maid had helped her wash and get dressed, opened the door into the parlour on the first floor. The smell of fresh coffee and warm bread greeted her first, and then, as she walked in, so did Bruise and Sam, both seated at a table set for six, with evidence four people had already eaten.

"Good morning, Miss Finnister!" Hubble, still wearing his hat, stood up. "So what d'you think of Mrs. Scott's establishment?"

"A grand secret, Bruise...who'd think, to look at the place, eh?"

"Exactly the point."

Josie looked at the two men. "You been out already?"

"We've been all over...up with the lark, if there was any left in these parts."

"You should've woke me."

"You was tired, girl...'sides, we're trying to keep you

a secret, too. Don't want that wossname Bland knowing yer here, do we?"

Josie sat down at the table. "Where've you been?"

"Out asking questions, making enquiries, just like them police do; only no one lies to us, do they, Sam?" Sam Baston smiled at the very thought.

"Did you find anything out?"

It was Hubble's turn to smile. "They're called Dooley and Husker."

"Who are?"

"The two what nabbed Daniel."

"Never heard of them." Josie reached across the table for a pot of coffee.

"They're staying at The Sun...heard of that?"

Standing out in the street, Daniel looked back at the building he'd just come out of. A dark curtain in one of the first-floor windows moved slightly and he thought he could make out a bony little hand: Old Meggy watching him. He turned and walked away.

And then, some way down the street, he stopped. Something was missing.

Daniel couldn't think what it could be – he had precious little to lose, after all – and then he realized what it was. The keys he'd taken from the cellar when he'd locked Dooley in the room were no longer in his jerkin pocket. Tom Ducato must have lifted them; like Old Meggy had said, he had the lightest fingers. But why would he want the keys?

Because Tom Ducato was, with every breath, a thief first and foremost.

And he more than likely thought the keys, the only thing of worth Daniel had on him, belonged to the place he'd seen him make a skulking exit from. If the Little Duke was anywhere it was back in the vicinity of The Sun that he'd probably find him now...wherever that was. Tom might think himself very clever, but Daniel was going to make him pay for playing him like a fool. They'd shaken hands, and if it was the last thing he did he was going to find Tom and make him do as he'd promised – he was going to take him to the only place Daniel could think to look for Mr. Hubble: The Ace.

## CHAPTER 18

# TURNING THE TABLES

The streets were crowded, reminding Daniel of busy days in any number of market towns when it seemed like everyone for miles around came traipsing to see the circus. Lots of people milling around didn't scare him in any way, but not knowing where he was made him feel very unsettled and ill at ease. His whole life had been spent moving from place to place, if not somewhere new every day then certainly every week, but always with the same faces...always with people he knew and trusted, people who would look after him no matter what. Which he couldn't say about anyone he'd met in London so far.

The sun was climbing ever higher in the sky and he thought it would be a perfect day if only he knew how to get back to The Sun. But he had no idea where the tavern was, how to get there, or if Tom was actually anywhere nearby; now, he thought to himself, would be a good time to "see the future", to know that what he was intending to do was the right thing.

Daniel took a deep, deep breath. What good was it to have this...ability, he supposed he could call it...this ability to see things before they happened if he couldn't control it? It was no good whatsoever. About as helpful as that Old Meggy looking at the tea leaves in the bottom of his cup. If he could control this thing he did, he'd know where Tom was, instead of standing on some street, as lost as a lamb. Although knowing did help, he realized; scary as the experience might be, seeing what was going to happen in that cellar room had spurred him on to find a way out. Because he'd believed it was possible.

He caught sight of himself in the window of a haberdasher's; reflected in the streaked, dusty glass was a face he hardly recognized, a dirty, tangle-haired boy with a wild look in his eyes. Tattered, on edge, weary. A far cry from the figure he cut in the circus ring as Crown Prince Juan Pablo, sitting astride the magnificent black Arab stallion Ozymandias. Daniel looked away, wondering if he'd ever be that person again. He could tell from the faces of the few people who happened to glance at him that he was little more to them than a stray dog loose on the street. They'd never believe he was, as the curtains drew apart and he appeared in the ring, *The Very Youngest Equestrian Master In This, Or Any Other Hemisphere!* Looking again at the person staring back at him from the window, he found it hard to believe himself.

"What d'you want, boy? Standing there, blocking the pavement, preventing decent customers from coming into my emporium!"

Daniel swung round. Standing in the open doorway of the haberdasher's was a tall, angular man, dark strands of hair plastered across his otherwise almost completely bald head, like they'd been drawn with a quill pen from just above his large right ear, all the way over to his equally prominent left one. He was peering at Daniel through a pair of small, wire-rimmed spectacles, his nose pinched, thin lips pursed tightly together and turned down.

"Well, boy?"

"I'm trying to find The Sun, it's a tavern—"

"I know what it is! I know what it is!" The man interrupted, leaning forward and making a show of looking up and down the street. "But is it here? No, it is not!" He waved dismissively. "So be off with you!"

"Tell me where it is and you'll never see me again."

"The very cheek! Bargaining?" The man looked behind him into the shop, as if wanting to find someone else to witness this extraordinary event, and then back down at Daniel. "I can hardly believe my ears!"

Daniel looked at him, thinking neither could he, the size of them. "Please, sir."

A frown creased the haberdasher's forehead, deep lines radiating out from the bridge of his nose, and he blinked. "An urchin with manners, who'd credit it, eh?" The man pushed away the thought with a shake of his head. "Well, boy, you are, by my reckoning, but a mere four or five minutes from your destination; run, and it would be less. Down this street, turn right into the main thoroughfare and take the second lane on the left. It's along there."

Daniel smiled the kind of smile he'd learned to put on for audiences when it was really the last thing he felt like doing. "Thank you."

No "sir" this time.

Walking away from the haberdasher's shop, Daniel was well aware of the man's beady little eyes following him down the street, checking he really was going. He realized now that Tom Ducato must have taken him on a purposefully confusing wild-goose chase – up hill and down dale, as Hannah would say – to Old Meggy's house; just another of the tricks he had to pay the "Little Duke" back for playing on him.

If he'd got it right, Daniel thought, Tom would likely be quite close to The Sun; he'd no doubt have the opinion that one of the keys might unlock a safe or a chest, which, for all Daniel knew, one of them did. If he'd any idea where Josie had hidden whatever it was she'd stolen from Carter Bland – and she surely must've taken something worth a king's ransom, considering the efforts he was making to get it back – Tom would be the perfect person to help him find it first.

But Daniel didn't know where Josie had hidden anything, although he'd bet a shiny sixpenn'orth it was more than likely somewhere in The Sun; somewhere she knew better than anywhere else. As he walked he thought for the first time about the strange turn of events that had brought him to this street in Clerkenwell, of how Josie's life and his had become entangled because he'd fallen asleep in her caravan, tired out after the fire. And what a tangle it was – him lost, her still being looked for by that Husker and Dooley, and a secret treasure waiting to be discovered.

On a corner, a ragged, shoeless boy was calling out to anyone who'd listen that the paper he was selling had within its pages all the latest news from the Crimea.

"Sebastopol still under siege!" he shouted, waving a copy of the papers he had over his arm at a passer-by. "Read all abaht it, guvnor – fresh off the press!"

"Call that news?" The man waved the urchin away. "I'll call it news when the damn thing's over and we've sent those blasted Russians packing!"

Turning away, the paper seller carried on yelling his wares and Daniel carried on his way, hoping against hope that Tom would still be in the vicinity of The Sun and not have moved on somewhere else, somewhere he'd never find him. What he'd give to have Seth and Jem with him now, the three of them would show that Little Duke a thing or two about rough justice. If there'd been three of them, they could split up and come at the tavern from different directions, quietly, like foxes in the night. But there was only him and he was just going to have to do this on his own.

Finding himself at the turning he had to take, down which he should find the tavern, if the sniffy haberdasher hadn't been lying to him, Daniel stopped. What next? He didn't want Tom to see him first (more, he did *not* want Husker, or Dooley if he'd been let out of the cellar, to see him at all), so he was going to have to be very careful. The one thing he had in his favour was the element of surprise, and he mustn't lose it.

Daniel stood leaning back against a wall and observed the general hubbub going on around him. Tradesmen and street sellers shouting about their various wares – the best songs, the very tastiest pies, the brightest matches you could ever wish for were all here. Residents hanging out of windows called to visitors and passers-by, everyone walking this way and that, the hot, listless air full of dust and smells, all sorts of smells. The aroma of baking bread and wood smoke mixing with the steam of horse droppings and the stink of whatever evil stew ran sluggishly down the gutters. Pungent enough to make your nose twitch, the reek of it served to remind Daniel that not only was he still hungry, but he also hadn't seen a wash rag for a day or so.

It was then he saw a hay cart making very slow progress down the street towards him, the driver yelling for people to make way for him, a request which seemed to fall mainly on deaf ears. As the cart approached the corner where Daniel was standing he saw the driver pull the reins and tap with his whip, telling the old nag it should start to turn. This could be just what he needed.

Daniel pushed himself off the wall and slunk towards the rear of the cart to take a look. His spirits rose when he saw the low, open back, covered in loose hay. After a quick glance left, right and behind him to check that no one was paying him any kind of serious attention, he dodged up to the cart, leaped forward and sideways, as if he was doing one of his tricks with Savage, instead rolling into the hay. Grabbing a loose sheaf he pulled some on top of himself and peered back out at the street. As far as he could tell, no one had noticed what he'd done (or, if they had, no one cared) and he now had a reasonable view, from his makeshift hiding place, of both sides of the street as the cart trundled down the cobblestones towards The Sun.

Breathing carefully so he didn't choke from the dust and chaff, Daniel's eyes darted from one side of the street to the other, searching the doorways and alleys, shadows and windows for any sign of the threadbare peaked cap under which he'd find Tom Ducato. The cart had rattled and jolted some little way past the tavern when he finally spotted him, not hiding at all but sitting as large and bold as you'd like on an empty wooden crate, smoking a small pipe.

As soon as enough people had moved between them, Daniel pushed the hay off himself and jumped back down onto the filthy street, running off into a narrow alleyway. Brushing pieces of straw from his trousers, he poked his head out of the alley and looked back to where Tom still sat, a wisp of pipe smoke rising lazily into the air above him. This was Daniel's moment and he'd better make the best use of it because it was unlikely to happen for him again...

Tom Ducato had no notion what hit him. One moment he was sitting enjoying a relaxing pipe of quite the sweetest tobacco – which, along with some fancy silk kerchiefs, a decent enough pocket watch and a bit of coin, he'd recently lifted off a couple of gentleman who were just slightly the worse for having had a few drinks – and the next he was being pulled off his makeshift seat, dragged by the scruff of his neck across the cracked paving stones and into an alley.

As he was dropped to the ground, gasping for breath, he looked up at his attacker, now silhouetted against the sliver of bright blue sky in between the buildings. He quickly ran through who it could be – someone he owed money to? There was no one he could think of. Was it maybe one of the men he'd so recently taken belongings from? He was never that careless to let anyone see him, and anyway this person was not so big. A rival dip, maybe, someone who thought this was his turf and wanted him off? A definite possibility, but...

"Hello, Tom...did you think I'd be that easy to get rid of?"

Tom propped himself up on one elbow. "Danny-boy? I was just coming back to get you..."

"You really think I was born yesterday, don't you? Taking me round the houses and leaving me with that old woman who's as much your mother as I am?"

Tom's answer was to deliver a swift, painful, hobnailed kick to Daniel's right shin and, as he staggered to one side, to make a run for it. The ploy nearly worked, but not quite. Daniel ignored the pain, lunged at Tom and dragged him backwards, landing a punch on his ear; incensed, Tom forgot about getting away and turned to face his tormentor.

"Want a fight, do you?"

Daniel licked his lips and nodded. "You need teaching a lesson, you do."

"Who, me?" Tom laughed. "Like to see you try."

Pretty sure he could take Tom, who might be older, but was smaller and slighter, Daniel saw the odds unexpectedly change against him as sunlight glinted off the thin, sharp blade Tom now held in his hand. It had appeared out of nowhere, like the magic tricks Comus could do, but it was real, he could see that. So this wasn't going to be a fair fight.

"Who's the teacher now, Danny-boy?"

Tensed and ready to react to any move Tom might make, Daniel tried to weigh up the situation, to work out if it was at all possible for him to get his own knife out before Tom stuck him like a pig. But there was no chance he'd be able to even get his hand in his pocket, let alone get the blade open, and there was nothing in the alley that he could use as a weapon, either.

Except, maybe...Daniel dropped to his knees and, an arm outstretched, feinted to the left and then fell to his right. Tom, knife to the front, moved in like a snake and took a handful of dust and dirt straight in the face. Daniel was up in a second, knocking the blade out of Tom's hand and kicking it back into the shadows behind him. This was more like it!

He swung at Tom, expecting to connect another punch, but his fist met only air; half blinded though he was, the snake had more moves left and Tom, head down and eyes streaming, ran into Daniel like a battering ram, knocking him to the ground. Winded, Daniel fought for breath as he rolled back up on his feet, desperate to stop Tom from lurching out into the street and getting away.

Even with tears streaming down his face from the dust in his eyes, Tom saw him coming and lashed out with another powerful kick, but this time Daniel was ready. He caught Tom's foot and sent him crashing to the ground, his cap flying off. By now Daniel wasn't really thinking what he was doing, just acting on instinct, and he wanted Tom to stay down, to be craven and apologetic. He leaped on him, pinning him to the ground.

"Had enough, Little Duke?"

In reply, Tom twisted like an uncoiling spring and Daniel suddenly found himself flat on his back, Tom's knees on his shoulders, Tom's fists pummelling like an engine. A glancing blow hit his lip and Daniel tasted blood as he struggled to shift the weight off him and return blows at the same time; this wasn't turning out to be the walkover he'd thought it would be, but the last thing he was going to do was give up. Never that. He'd have to be knocked senseless before this fight was going to stop.

For a second Tom sat back. "*You* had enough, Your Bloomin' Highness?"

"No!" Daniel took his chance. Straining forward to get his shoulders as far off the ground as he could, he then rocked back down and whipped his legs up and around Tom's neck in a scissor-like movement which completely took Tom by surprise and left the boy powerless to do anything. "D'you give up...want to cut the rope now?"

The only sound was the hiss and wheeze of Tom trying to breathe.

Daniel tightened his grip, watching Tom's hands,

frozen in mid-air. "All I want's a truce – that, and for you to stop treating me like a stupid rustic and take me to somewhere called The Ace."

Still nothing.

"Well, what d'you say?" Daniel's legs gripped harder. "Friends for as long as it takes to get me there, and no hard feelings? Or..."

"*Or what?*" A tense, hoarse whisper.

"Why chance it?" Daniel reached up and took Tom's right hand. "Shake?"

"*Shake...*"

Very slowly, Daniel uncurled his legs from around Tom's neck, while Tom gradually straightened his legs, pulling Daniel off the ground as he got up. They stood, still gripping hands, and eyed each other.

"A deal's a deal, right Tom? No going back?"

Tom grinned. "Trust me!"

Daniel let go of Tom's hand. *Trust?* he thought. *Not likely!*

# CHAPTER 19
# STEPS IN THE RIGHT DIRECTION

Josie, aware the table was being cleared of the remnants of breakfast and more food brought in, sat and listened as Hubble told her what he and Sam Baston had been doing and what they'd found out. Platters of cold meat, two large roast chickens, a selection of pies, pitchers of beer, a plate of butter and a basket of loaves of bread were set down. Enough, thought Josie, to feed a small army.

*"So stop stuffing your face for a moment and tell me what they said!"*

Hubble cut himself a slice of bread three fingers thick, tore a leg off one of the chickens and cut a quarter out of a pie. "Truth of the matter is, Josie, the more people dislike a person, the more they'll tell you about what that person is up to. And there are folk to be found what surely hate that Carter Bland."

"Who've you been talking to?"

"Bodies what work for the man..." Most of the slice of pie disappeared in one bite. "We watched The Ace and followed a few of them after they left, got talking at the inn they went to for a measure before going home. Mark my words, a sympathetic ear and a couple of glasses of porter will open mouths like keys do doors."

"So stop stuffing your face for a moment and tell me what they said!" Josie tapped the table impatiently with her knuckle.

Hubble took a long, slow sip of beer. "We are reliably informed that those two – the ones I told you about, Dooley and Husker – came into The Ace very late last night. Dooley had something slung over his shoulder, which the man Husker made him carry more 'ladylike'...that's what he was heard to say."

"They still thought they'd got me?"

"Appears so." Hubble poured himself more beer.

Sam reached over and took the second leg from the chicken Hubble had started work on. "The one man say he hear shoutin' later, from the room upstair. Lotta shoutin'."

Josie's face dropped. "Don't fret." Hubble leaned across the table and patted her hand. "Far as we know, Daniel's still alive – we think they took him back to The Sun."

Before Josie had a chance to say anything else there was a knock on the door and one of the maids came in and bobbed to Mr. Hubble. "Mrs. Scott says there's some gennelmen come to see you and do you want them sent up now, sir?"

"Are they all here, Kitty?"

"I couldn't say, Mr. Hubble, sir, as I don't know how many you might be expecting. But there's five or six downstairs now, sir."

"Send 'em up, Kitty."

A couple of minutes later there were half a dozen more people sitting and standing round the table and making short work of the food laid out on it. Must be the small army the spread was intended for, thought Josie, as she watched the proceedings; and a motley crew they were too. A more ragtag bunch it'd be hard to imagine, this collection of shifty, battle-scarred men who'd all very obviously got to where they were by travelling the hardest of roads.

She'd recognized two of them – Vinnie Staver and Tod Bell – as occasional customers at The Sun and thought she'd maybe heard of another man, but the others were strangers to her; they'd all introduced themselves as they came into the room, and, despite what they looked like, were politeness itself. But she could tell these were men who cared nothing for anyone's laws and for whom life, other people's at least, was cheap. What connected each and every person in the room was their obvious and deep respect for the old bare-knuckle fighter holding court up at the head of the table, swapping stories as he gnawed on a chicken leg.

Josie watched and waited, wanting this strange meeting – called for reasons she didn't yet understand – to begin, but knowing that it wasn't her place to say or do anything. These were Bruise's people and everything should be done his way. And then, finally, Hubble rapped hard on one of the pitchers with the back of a knife to bring the meeting to order. Conversations petered out and all eyes turned to Hubble as he stood up.

"You've all come, even though you don't know why I asked you here – and for that I thank everyone now. A couple of you have already rolled their sleeves up and been busy." Hubble nodded at Vinnie Staver and Tod Bell. "The rest will find out exactly what I have in mind shortly. Begging your indulgence a moment or two longer, gentlemen, I'd like to hear from Vinnie and Tod what news they have. Vinnie?"

Vinnie coughed, pushing long, greasy locks of curly black hair out of his face and wiped the back of his hand across his mouth. "He was in The Sun, Bruise, like what you said, but the lad ent there no more."

Josie bolted forward in her chair. "Not there, but..." She saw Vinnie frowning at her and sat back, blushing slightly.

Hubble waved away the interruption. "Where've they took him now, then?"

"Took him nowhere, Bruise...seems the lad excaped."

Hubble frowned and shot a glance at Josie. "Daniel did – how so?"

"Don't know as to exackly how, but Jess, one of the skivvy-girls we got talking to," Josie nodded that she knew who Vinnie was talking about, "she said the lad somehow managed to knock that Dooley character senseless and lock him up. Took the keys with him, which meant his partner had to shoot the lock to get the good-for-nothing out!"

Tod, his dirty blond hair not quite covering a raw scar that ran from forehead to ear and pulled his right eyelid down, looked over at Josie. "The girl said she saw him, must've been just as he'd got out the cellar.

Said she give him the all-clear to hightail it out the yard, there being no one there." He turned to look at Hubble. "We give her a couple of coins... Sounds a top cove, your boy, Bruise."

"Did the girl say where he might be going?" Hubble asked.

Tod shook his head.

"What about the blockhead and his friend, wossname, Husker, any news of them?"

"One of the pot-boys said Husker'd come back in a foul mood, then left almost as soon as he'd got there, and in a worse one...took Dooley with him, calling him all the names under the sun for a dolt, and then some." Tod speared a thick piece of ham. "Word is, they've been sent back to find Miss Finnister here."

Hubble smiled. "And good luck to 'em, I say."

"Daniel would've been safer if he'd stayed put, eh, Bruise?" Josie nervously chewed her lip.

"How was he to know we'd find him so quick?" Hubble said. "We'll just have to hope he keeps his wits about him and watches who he falls in with."

Daniel stood by the stone horse trough Tom had taken him to; his lip still stung and he felt bruised in quite a lot of places, but nothing hurt too badly. He'd dunked his head in the murky water and was now smoothing back his wet hair, wiping his face and watching as Tom did the same. He knew he couldn't trust this boy, whose whole life was thieving and dishonesty, but he had little choice in who to ask for help. Then Tom, his cap and jacket on the ground by his feet, came up for air.

"Are you really going to help me?"

Tom blinked at Daniel. "Me? Said I would dint I?"

"But..."

"Shook hands, too." Tom rubbed his face, using his jacket as a towel. "So like I said, trust me."

"You've heard of the place where I want to go?"

"Ace of Clubs?" Tom grinned. "Course I have, and I know where it is, too...there can be rich pickings round places like that, specially when a winner's had more'n enough to drink! Why'd *you* want to go there, though?"

"It's the one place I can think of where I might meet up with the people looking for me."

Tom glanced at Daniel, giving him a look. "He must be a fancy bloke with plenty of actual to throw around, your Mr. Hubble, if he's going in a place like that."

"He ain't rich." Daniel returned the look, knowing Tom was probably making assumptions about the size of tip he might get for taking him to The Ace. "And he ain't going in to gamble neither."

* * *

They must, Tom had insisted as they'd walked away from the trough, go back to Old Meggy's before he could take Daniel over to where The Ace was. He had to get rid of the silk kerchiefs and the watch (which was a credit to its makers as, astonishingly, it had survived the fight in remarkably good condition, considering). There was no point, he'd said, in carrying booty around when you could have the money for it.

On the way back, each with half of a still-warm pie Tom had bought from a street seller, they went past the haberdasher's shop, the owner still at the door, waiting for customers. When they got to Old Meggy's, Daniel stopped as Tom went up to the door.

"Not coming in?"

"She doesn't like me."

"Old Meg don't like no one too much...come on." Tom opened the door and went in without waiting to see if Daniel was following him.

Looking up and down the street he finally entered the building. Better to be with Tom than to let him out of his sight so he could do another runner. Better by far. Daniel found Tom outside Old Meg's door, waiting. "She not in?"

"She's always in, never not here," Tom rapped on the door again, "not ever...Meggy! It's Little Duke!"

The door finally opened a crack. "You got something nice for Old Meggy this time, not just some hungry child needs feeding and eats up all me food and doesn't give me nothing for it in return?"

"I got something."

"What?"

"Some silk and a ticker, Meggy, lovely stuff."

The door opened a few more inches and Daniel saw the old woman's hand beckoning. "Is it silver, Duke? Did you get me silver?"

Tom shook his head. "Plate or pinchbeck, Meggy. But the silk's true enough."

As Old Meggy opened the door to let Tom in she saw Daniel. "What's he back here for? I told him to be on his way!"

"I'm just taking him up West, Meggy, said I would."

"You are, are you...well tell him to stay outside...he's a strange one." She peered out, squinting at Daniel and shaking her head. "I saw things in his cup, I did."

Tom looked back over his shoulder at Daniel, then down at Old Meg. "What things?"

The old woman started muttering to herself distractedly and Daniel couldn't make out what she was saying at first. She was going on and on about what she'd seen in his tea leaves, and he realized she'd said something about his mother, and his brother, and then he caught what sounded like the word "queen". His mother was a queen – did she *really* think he was Prince Juan Pablo?

"You, boy, I knew it when I first saw you!" Pointing, her bony finger shaking, Old Meggy looked Daniel up and down in a way that made it appear she was nervous of him. "You've got the eye, boy, you've got the eye... now I see you again, I'm sure of it – you stay there, boy, don't set a foot across my threshold!" She grabbed Tom's sleeve, pulling him down towards her and whispering loudly. *"He's got the eye!"*

Glancing at Daniel, Tom pushed Old Meggy into the room and went after her, slamming the door shut and leaving Daniel alone on the landing, wondering what on earth the old witch had meant. Did her saying he had "the eye" mean she knew about what he could do, that he could see things that later happened? But she couldn't know...Comus was the only person he'd ever really talked to about it, so how *could* she know? Daniel felt apprehensive. He didn't like this place, this damp, rotten house, it made him feel uneasy, made him feel it didn't like him either.

He wanted to go back to the only home he'd ever known, which, though it wasn't built out of bricks and mortar, was always warm and welcoming. He felt a loneliness moving over him, like a cold mist, a sense of loss that made him feel like he was slowly fading away. Who was he without his circus family round him?

To find them he had to first get back to The Ace, because it was the place where everything had started; Josie had stolen something terribly important from there, and it was where Dooley and Husker had brought him, where the evil Carter Bland sat, like a spider at the centre of its web. Daniel could only hope it would be the place where things might come to an end.

Mr. Hubble *would* come looking for him, he had to believe that was true because he had nothing else left to cling to, and where else would he start looking but The Ace? All Daniel could think of was that he had to be there, waiting, for when Mr. Hubble came. What other options did he have?

"Danny-boy."

Daniel had been miles away and hadn't heard the door open; he focused on Tom, now back out on the landing. "Yes?"

"Let's go."

# CHAPTER 20
# ONWARD

Tom turned and stood in front of Daniel as they came out of the house. "What did you say to Old Meggy when I left you there before?"

"Me? Nothing...why?"

"Must've said something, she was going on like some mad old Bedlam crone and give me better than fair money for my stuff, too, and no argy-bargy. Not like herself at all." Tom shrugged and started walking. "Kept on about you having the eye and that she saw these things, like what she said, in yer tea leaves...not Irish, are you? Look like you could be, black hair and that."

Daniel shook his head. "Don't know...like I told you, I'm adopted, no idea who my real parents are."

"Have you got the eye?"

"What d'you mean?"

Tom stopped and stuck out his right hand and held up a small sixpenny coin in the other. "I'll cross yer palm with silver and you tell me what the future holds, gypsy boy."

Daniel kept on walking. "I'm *not* a gypsy."

"Well you played some sort of tricksy thing on Old Meggy that brought Little Duke some good luck today, Danny-boy, so I shall now escort you to where you want to go!" Tom caught Daniel up and then walked, matching him pace for pace. "Tell me why it is you want to go to a fancy gambling house then – you got money hidden on you I haven't found yet?"

"No."

"You're a mystery, you are, a regular poser."

Daniel didn't want to be a mystery. He wanted to get back to the circus, he wanted to do the things he'd always done, the things he was good at doing. He did not want to be walking down a dingy, narrow London street with this chancer who'd likely sell his own mother, if he had one.

"Where is your mother then, if it's not Old Meggy?"

"She died, years ago." Tom flicked the small silver coin in the air and caught it. "Bad air, bad water, bad something it was that got her; bad gin most likely, from what I can remember."

"Sometimes..." Daniel stopped talking.

"Sometimes what?"

"I wonder why my mother didn't want me...why she left me where she did."

"And where was that, Danny-boy?"

"In the lion's cage."

"Never!"

"It's true. That's why I'm called Daniel, like the story in the Bible."

"And I'm called Thomas after St Thomas Aquinas, because he was born in Naples, like my father's father. So my mother said."

"How long ago did she die, your mother?"

"Don't remember, but not long after my old man went and left us."

Daniel glanced at Tom, a boy as much of an orphan as he was, but with none of the family Daniel realized he'd been lucky enough to have been given instead. All Tom had was Old Meggy. The two boys carried on walking side by side, each lost in their own thoughts. It was Tom who finally broke the silence.

"Can you really see things?"

Daniel kicked a small stone into the gutter and nodded.

"Do it now, Danny-boy, do it now and tell me what I'll be." Tom nudged him with his elbow. "Do I ever get to be a real duke, or is Newgate Prison and a hanging end what I've got to look forward to?"

"It just happens to me...I see these things that come true later, I see people I've never met before, and I don't know why. But I can't *make* it happen, it just does."

Tom grabbed Daniel's wrist and held him, looking him straight in the eye. "You could try, couldn't you? For me?"

Daniel stared back at Tom, a kind of tingling shiver running up his arm from where Tom's hand tightly gripped him. He knew this feeling, it had happened before...then Daniel blinked and for the very shortest of moments the street sounds changed and he saw a man standing in front of him and he knew it was Tom. Smartly dressed and quite tall, with a brilliant diamond pin sparkling in his silk cravat, he smiled Tom's wide smile at someone, winked and then...and then Daniel found himself looking at the Little Duke, still holding his wrist, a puzzled expression on his face.

"What happened, Danny-boy? I thought you'd turned to stone there – did you see something?"

"I..." Daniel didn't know what to say, had no notion

what the vision he'd seen really meant. "I didn't see the gallows, Tom. I saw a diamond, but I didn't see the gallows..."

The air was still thick with tobacco smoke, the table covered in empty plates and glasses, but there were now just three people in the room on the second floor of Mrs. Scott's establishment in Monmouth Street. The meeting had been over for some five minutes and Mr. Hubble had called for a fresh pot of coffee. Josie stood up and walked stiffly to the window; sniffing, she parted the lace curtains and looked out.

Hubble and Sam Baston stopped talking and glanced at each other, both finally realizing that there might be something Josie was not happy about; Hubble made a silent, questioning face at Sam, who, eyes widened, mouth turned down, shook his head in reply. Hubble coughed.

"You all right there, Josie-girl?"

"I most certainly am not, James Hubble." Josie turned round, an angry red blush on her cheeks.

"Oh...and why might that be?"

"It might well be because *all* I am to do tonight is keep my own company while the world is set to rights on my behalf!"

Hubble frowned. "I'm not sure as I follow."

"Right here in this room – while I sat and listened and was mostly ignored as if I was no more than a piece of furniture – you make all your plans and when I *do* say something you all pay as much attention to me as you would if I were the lowest skivvy-maid."

As if on cue there was a knock on the door and Kitty brought in the pot of coffee Hubble had asked for.

"Would you like the table cleared now, Mr. Hubble, sir?"

"No, Kitty, later will do." Hubble smiled and nodded, then turned back to Josie. "I still don't follow."

Josie, bristling with barely contained anger, waited for the maid to leave and then took a deep breath. "This is all more to do with me than anyone who was here – it's all *my* fault Daniel got kidnapped, and it's *my* fight with Carter Bland as it was me what overheard the conversation and stole the documents and ran away. Right?"

Hubble didn't say anything.

"And there you go, telling these three here," Josie indicated some empty chairs at the table, "to go to The Sun and get back the papers I hid there, and then you tell the others to meet you later near The Ace so you can go in and deal with Bland. What about me, Bruise, what am *I* supposed to be doing when all this is going on? Darning your socks?"

"What we have to do isn't business for women to be involved in, nor is it going to be done by people women should be dealing with; ruffians is going to be seeing to thugs tonight." Hubble reached over to pour some coffee.

"Just a minute." Josie walked back to the table. "Now are you *quite* sure I shouldn't be doing that, being as how I'm *just* a woman?"

Hubble sat back. "Pour me coffee, if you want, but you must stay here. If your father, rest his soul, was alive and heard I wasn't looking after his only girl, he'd bloody my nose."

"But he's dead, Bruise, and Carter Bland as good as made that happen as well. I've a right to be there."

Hubble drained his coffee cup and stood up. "Not to my way of thinking. Look lively, Mr. Baston, we have work to do."

Stunned, Josie watched the two men make for the door. "And what's to stop me finding my own way?"

Hubble looked over his shoulder. "The watch I've had put on this place..."

Tom waited for enough of a gap in the seemingly endless parade of growlers, carts, buses and carriages filling the street and dashed across to the other side, Daniel following close behind him. He wasn't used to this amount of hustle and bustle on the roads; when the circus paraded through the towns and villages they visited, the streets became theirs and everything stopped for them; Daniel, riding Savage, often led the way at the head of the column. Dodging hooves and wheels was not a trick he'd had to learn.

They'd been walking for some time, Daniel ever watchful of Tom and what he might do next; he seemed to treat the journey they were making as a huge opportunity, constantly making little forays here and there, to do what, Daniel didn't ask. The road he saw just up ahead, which crossed at right angles the street they were walking down, appeared to act like a natural border between the poor and the rich, the teeming rookeries and slums they were passing through on one side, and what looked like finer buildings and fancier people on the other.

"What's down there?" Daniel nodded ahead.

"Oxford Street. One day I'll have made enough money to be able to walk along there and go about my business like a real gent."

The picture of the man with Tom's smile and the big diamond flashed across Daniel's mind, as if to prove the truth of what his companion was wishing for. "You never been caught?"

"Had some close shaves, some *very* close shaves, but Little Duke's been a lucky cove – so far!"

"Aren't you scared of being caught? If they don't string you up, they'll likely send you off, never to be seen again."

"I'd take transportation over the rope any day..." Tom stopped walking and moved over to lean against a building.

Daniel followed, eyes darting left and right. "What's the matter, you seen something?"

"Nothing, but we've got to be careful from now on. The likes of you and me, we aren't so welcome where you want to go, and the rozzers ain't half quick to use their boots. 'Kick you as soon as look at you' is their motto, in my experience. We'll have to find somewhere decent to put ourselves to do the watching, if we want to be left alone."

After a careful saunter round the environs where The Ace of Clubs was situated, Tom finally delivered the opinion that they'd do best if they found a place where they could keep a good watch on the back entrance. Daniel was puzzled as to why the back and not the front.

"Your Mr. Hubble – that his name?" Daniel nodded. "He a toff?"

The question made Daniel smile, because if there was anyone who was less of a dandy than Mr. Hubble, he'd like to meet them. "No, you'd never call him that."

"Then I doubt he'd be let in the front – did you catch the types going inside? If your man doesn't know it already, he'll find out pretty soon that round the tradesmen's is where he belongs. Delivering."

As they walked back round to one of the narrow alleys which led to the rear of The Ace, the more Daniel thought about it, the more logical the plan seemed and the more glad he was that Tom – even if it was just that he was hoping to be paid – had come with him.

The small lane the rear of The Ace let on to was no easy place to find somewhere decent to hide, as they had to be extremely careful they weren't noticed doing the looking. In the end it was Daniel who spotted the slightly open door in a small wooden outhouse not so very far away from the gate leading to The Ace's yard. The shack was empty, it was dry and there was a reasonable view if you left the door open an inch or two.

But it was also dark, hot and airless, and both boys were tired. It was hard to say who nodded off first, but an hour or so after setting up to keep a watch, they were both fast asleep.

# CHAPTER 21
# THE TIME HAS COME

They arrived one at a time. The four men who had been in the room on the second floor of Mrs. Scott's walked into The Lantern tavern and kept their own individual company, with no more than a small nod in the direction of James Hubble and Sam Baston, sitting at a table over by the unlit fireplace.

You couldn't tell, but each man was a veritable walking arsenal of weaponry – cudgels, saps and pistols, all well hidden under coats that, if you'd thought about it, were a mite on the heavy side for an August evening. But it didn't do to pay too close attention to Tye Brookes, Henry Grey, Kit Pullman and Walt Forde, so no one did. And everyone breathed a little easier when the last of the six strangers had left the inn.

The plans had all been made and each man knew what was expected of him. The first to peel away from the loose group was Tye Brookes, disappearing down an unnamed side street. With the dusk turning to night, and before the lamplighters had got all the street lamps burning, Henry Grey and Walt Forde split off next and walked away, slowly picking up their pace till they turned the corner ahead at a trot.

Hubble and Kit Pullman strolled along, looking like nothing more than a pair of old friends out for an early evening constitutional; behind them strode Sam Baston, with what light there was left reflecting dully off his smooth skin.

Minutes later the three of them came into a square with a small, iron-fenced garden in the centre, dark now as the street lights here weren't yet lit. Henry Grey and Walt Forde had done their job well, bribing, or scaring, the lamplighters to give the square a miss for the next hour or so; the dark best suited a certain type of work. There were lights to be seen in some of the windows where curtains had yet to be been drawn and over to their left the men could see twin gas lamps, one either side of a wide dark-red door, making its large, polished brass handle glint as if it was on fire. The Ace of Clubs, in all its glory.

Hubble nodded and they crossed the road and went into the garden, its cast-iron gate unlocked; another of Henry and Walt's little jobs seen to. Walking along the path that took them over to the entrance opposite The Ace, Hubble whistled a high then a low note, getting first one reply and then a second; he and Kit stopped in the shadows, waiting for Henry and Walt to join them. Then he cracked his knuckles, one by one.

"Gentlemen, we have business to attend to..."

Sam Baston reached up, easily able to grip and turn off the gas tap for the lamps on either side of the club's front door. Hubble nodded, brought a short, heavy club out of his coat and rapped on the door with it. As the door began to open, Sam Baston earned his name of The Mighty Ox as all seventeen stone of hard, strongman muscle rammed into the heavy door and smashed it into whoever was standing inside, knocking him senseless. Sam carried on into The Ace's marbled foyer, followed by Hubble, who swung a windmill punch at the man who'd come out of the cloakroom to see what the commotion was all about; Hubble's fist had lost none of the power he'd been famous for in his prizefighting days, and the man he hit fell to the floor and stayed there.

As soon as Sam made his move, the other three men were across the road in a flash. Once inside, Kit Pullman secured the door with its bolts, drew the curtains of the windows either side of it and then, taking out his Colt Navy six-shot revolver, stood guard while Henry and Walt helped drag the two unconscious footmen into the cloakroom to tie and gag them.

Hubble stood in the middle of the floor, breathing deeply, and took stock of the situation. They were inside, and not a shot had been fired. Yet. They controlled the front entrance and had Tye Brookes at the rear of the building, covering the back way in and out. He'd been told to stay put unless he heard gunfire, and only then to come inside.

Hubble had chosen this hour to strike as it was early, and there probably wouldn't be many people at the gaming tables; the only people they'd have to deal with were the odd client who might get uppity (and there was nothing worse than a bad loser for making trouble), and the coves whose job it was to protect the money. As soon as they realized what was happening, that would be when things began to get interesting.

"Kit, stay here with Henry...lock up anyone who comes this way and plug the first one who don't do what he's told as a lesson to the rest. In the leg, mind, unless they try to get you first. Walt, get yer shooter out and let's go and find Mr. Carter Bland."

Before she'd discovered she wasn't included in the plans, Josie had drawn a rough sketch of The Ace, to show where in the building they would find Carter Bland. The quickest way, she'd said, was up the main stairs to the second floor and then along a wide corridor that had private gaming rooms on either side of it. They'd find him where he always was when the place was open for business, in one of the two adjoining rooms at the back.

Following the younger men up the central staircase, Hubble smiled. This reminded him so much of when he was in his prime and scaring up a fight was what he did for others' entertainment as well as his own. Personally, he couldn't wait to mix it with whoever was supposed to be looking after this place and, in a funny sort of way, he hoped that finding Bland wouldn't be too easy.

On the first landing his wish was granted.

As Walt was starting up the second flight of stairs a door opened on the other side of the landing behind them. Hubble turned to see a tall, broad-shouldered, bullish young man – dark hair cut close to his head and thin stiletto sideburns running down his cheeks; the man closed the door behind him and turned, frowning at the sight of three armed ruffians acting as if the place belonged to them.

"Oi!" he shouted, pointing. "And just who d'you think you lot are?"

Hubble strode over towards the man, wearing as friendly an expression as he could muster on his battered face, and stopped in front of him; the man waited, appearing to think this large shambling figure approaching him was about to explain himself, but instead Hubble clouted him with a solid uppercut. The man fell like a tree.

"Wiped his chops good and proper there, Bruise." Walt started to come back down the stairs. "What d'you want to do with him?"

Hubble was about to ask Sam to move the body out of sight when the landing door opened again and two more men appeared, momentarily stunned by the scene playing out in front of them. Then one leaped at Hubble, fists flying, while the other drew a short-barrelled revolver and waved it threateningly at Sam and then at Walt.

"Stop right there, the both of you, or I'll shoot!"

Walt, who reckoned the man looked like he wasn't up to much when it came to guns, didn't think twice; swinging his right arm up, he aimed and fired a single shot, the hefty recoil kicking his hand up. "Don't say what yer going to do, *do* what yer going to do," he muttered, as Sam prised the man off Hubble and slammed him face first into the wall.

"And *I* said to shoot 'em in the *leg*, not the head – is he dead, Sam?"

Sam stepped over to the man lying crumpled on the floor in front of him, blood streaming out of a wound above his left ear; he bent down, reaching out to feel for a pulse, then stood up, shaking his head. "Musta got hisself a proper thick skull, Bruise."

Daniel woke with a start, slumped against the side of the small wooden shed, his head lolling forward. It was, to his utter amazement, almost pitch-black outside and for a moment he had no idea where he was. Then everything came flooding back – they were supposed to be keeping a watch on the back of The Ace!

*They*...where was Tom, had he gone and left him?

"Are you there, Tom?" Daniel got up gingerly, his legs and backside numb, pins and needles in his feet.

There was a rustling noise to Daniel's left and someone groaned.

"Lord help us, what did we go and do? Is it night out there or am I gone completely blind?"

"We fell asleep, Tom."

"Did you just wake?"

"I did, but I think it was because I heard something."

"What?"

"Maybe I was dreaming, but I swear it was a pistol shot."

"Can you see anything outside?"

"Haven't looked."

Tom, who was nearest the door, got up off the ground; he could now just make out the sliver of grey in the darkness that must be where the door was slightly open and he shuffled over to it. Gently pushing it away from him a few more inches, he stuck his head out and as he did so the moon appeared from behind a bank of clouds and there, in the night shadows of a small rowan tree some few yards away, he saw a figure, hiding.

"*There's someone out there!*" Tom ducked back into the shed, speaking low in an excited whisper. "*Come and see...*"

Daniel made to join him, but tripped over something on the floor and stumbled heavily into Tom, who had just leaned forward to take another look outside. Both boys lost their balance and tumbled out of the shed, landing in a heap of arms and legs on the ground. Tom was the first to get to his feet, staying low and swinging round to check what the person he'd seen was doing, ready at any moment to make a run for it. What he saw as the figure moved out of the shadows took him totally by surprise.

"It's a moll, Danny-boy!"

Daniel rolled up on to his feet. "What?"

"Y'know...a woman!"

Taking another step or two, her face still in the shadows cast by her bonnet, the woman spoke. "Daniel? Is that you?"

Daniel's mouth fell open. "Josie?"

"Who's this, Danny-boy? 'Cos it surely ain't no Mr. Hubble."

Josie stepped forward. "It's me all right, Daniel, but what the *devil* are you doing hiding out here?"

"Came to wait for Mr. Hubble, as I thought, if he was going to be looking for me, which he surely would, this is maybe where he'd start. What are *you* doing here, all on your own – where's Mr. Hubble?"

"He left me behind, went off with Sam Baston and some others and said it wasn't the work for a woman to be doing. Put a guard on the place we're staying at and everything. But I wanted to be here, to spit in that Carter Bland's face when they got him."

Tom, still standing back a bit, eyes narrowed

suspiciously, butted in. "How'd you get out, then, if the place was all guarded up?"

"Who's this, Daniel?"

"It's Tom, Tom Ducato...he helped me find my way here, said he'd stay with me till I found Mr. Hubble."

Tom and Josie looked each other over, still keeping their distance, experience not allowing either one to trust the other. Josie had a fair idea of the type of boy Tom was, and Tom knew it. It was as fascinating as watching a cat warily circle a dog, but there were more important things to be doing than that.

"Was it a shot I heard, Josie?" Daniel blurted out.

Josie glanced at him, frowning. "A shot? Yes, I think so... I was about to go and take a closer look when you two appeared out of nowhere."

"Well, shall we go and take a closer look now?" Daniel started to move towards The Ace's back entrance.

"You should stay here, Daniel. Bruise'll not be happy if I bring you with me."

"You won't leave me here; I'm coming in!"

"So am I," chimed in Tom. Glancing at Josie, Tom leaned over towards Daniel. "More than likely," he whispered, "there's something in there that'll pay me well for bringing you here."

"What's going on with you two?"

“Nothing, ma’am,” Tom smiled, “nothing at all.”

“He was just saying that, well...” Daniel shrugged, “...you’ll be safer in there with us two along.” He could feel himself blushing at the lie, but he really did feel he owed a debt to Tom for getting him to The Ace, and guilty that he had no money to pay the debt off – and if Tom took something of Carter Bland’s, was that *such* a bad thing? The thought took Daniel by surprise and he shot a look at Tom; maybe he’d been spending too much time in bad company...

# CHAPTER 22
# ROUGH JUSTICE

Josie, pulled this way and that, finally gave in and agreed to let Daniel and Tom come with her into The Ace. Hubble was going to be angry enough that she'd disobeyed him and used the hidden, underground passage – which a shilling or two had easily persuaded the maid, Kitty, to tell her about. The secret escape route, at the disposal of certain residents whenever they felt it was advisable they shouldn't use the more normal ways in and out, went from behind a dresser in the cellar of Mrs. Scott's establishment and came up in a house two streets away.

What Bruise would say when he saw she'd brought Daniel with her was no one's business, and as for the young jackanapes he'd got with him, she didn't trust that boy not even as far as she could throw him, but she could see Daniel wanted him to come with them. Part of her, she had to admit, felt better having these two with her as she pushed open the door to The Ace's backyard and slipped inside. The idea of going into the place on her own had made her heart beat like a monkey on a drum. Josie looked behind her and saw Tom quietly closing the door.

"Keep to the shadows, lads."

"This ain't me first time, lady."

"He's never been caught, Josie."

Josie nodded to herself, not surprised by either piece of information, and carried on up the pathway that led to the back door. It was open, which was nothing unusual, except she knew that the man who'd been introduced to her as Tye Brookes was supposed to be here, somewhere, guarding it. She took a deep breath and started up the back steps; in this part of The Ace she was only likely to meet kitchen staff and others who wouldn't have many good words to say about Carter Bland. Even if they'd heard she'd gone missing and that he was looking for her, she was pretty sure they'd keep mum.

It was those bull-baiters in their fancy tailcoats, who smiled at the ladies and nodded to the gentlemen players, but would muscle anyone who caused trouble at the tables out through the door and into a hansom as quick as blinking. They were the ones she had to worry about.

Reaching the top of the steps, Josie stopped. "Keep with me, and if it looks like trouble, run like Hell." Turning to walk into the building, she took out of her bag the tiny, pearl-handled Derringer pistol which had been her father's. She might be just a girl, but she was a girl with the means to fight back...

There was no time to lose now, and Hubble knew it. The amount of fuss and disturbance they'd made – the fight, the gunfire and all – would have alerted everyone with ears to the fact that something was most definitely up in this place. Walt and Sam had taken the stairs two at a time and he was making his way after them at his own, slightly more leisurely pace; he now had his pistol out because, even though he was much happier to put up his dukes and fight, Hubble knew having a gun in your hand under these circumstances was by far the most sensible option.

Hubble could hear Walt and Sam running down the corridor and as he made the top landing the sound of a door being slammed was followed by a thud that Hubble felt through the soles of his boots, and then came the loud splintering of wood. Turning into the corridor he could see one of the doors at the end had been smashed open and thought to himself, who needed keys when you had Baron Magnus, The Mighty Ox?

On this floor The Ace seemed to be strangely quiet, like the building was holding its breath, and then, as he walked towards what he had to presume were Carter Bland's rooms – if he'd understood Josie's diagram correctly – Hubble heard a door being surreptitiously opened behind him and someone coughed.

"My good man..."

Hubble stopped walking, but didn't turn round. "I'm not, and never will be that, sir," he said. In the silence he glanced sideways and, letting his right hand fall down, he pulled back the hammer and cocked the pistol. "My advice to you, sir, is to get back to your game; act deaf, dumb and blind to anything else and you'll likely wake up tomorrow a happier man than what you'll be if you don't."

As the door behind him closed with a soft click, Hubble carried on walking down the corridor. Reaching the end he went into the room, large splinters crunching underfoot, and tried to push the door further back, but its buckled hinges protested and refused to move. The place was empty.

"Sam? Walt?"

"We're here, Bruise, in the next room. Sam's got the feller battened down nicely."

Hubble went through into the adjoining room to find Walt covering Sam Baston, who was holding Carter Bland in an armlock. The man looked like a scared rag doll in his grip.

Hubble went behind the brass-bound desk and sat down, putting his pistol in front of him on the polished green leather. "So you're Mr. Carter Bland...I wondered what a lickspittle weasel might look like."

"Who are you...what...what d'you want?" Bland's face, a picture of equal parts fright, pain and confusion, was pale and he'd broken out into a sweat; running through his mind were two thoughts: what were these men going to do to him, and where in God's name were his boys? This could not be happening to him! "Is it money? You can have what's here, except it won't be much as it's too early...hardly anyone's here yet."

Hubble smiled and shook his head. "You think everything's about readies, don't you, Mr. Bland? Well let me tell you, it ain't. I don't want your dirty money, none of it. And when we leave here, my friends and me, we won't be taking nothing with us but you.

"Walt, take a look outside and check nothing untoward's happening. We'll be bringing our man down shortly and we don't want no more trouble than we have to have, now do we."

Frowning, Bland's right eye twitched as he watched Walt leave the room. "What's going on? Where are you taking me?"

"Your sort, you never get proper justice for your crimes. Too good for justice, too high and mighty to be bound by the law, you are." Hubble sat forward, a serious expression on his face, and leaned his elbows on the desk. "'Cepting this time there will be judgement, mark my words."

"Crimes? What crimes? This is as honest a gaming house as you'll find in London!"

"That I doubt...but this is not about your crooked games." Hubble picked up the revolver and pointed it at Bland, whose eye twitched even more as he cringed. "It's about kidnap and treason and your dealings with a certain Mr. – what did Josie say was his name, Sam?"

"Nakhimov, Bruise." Sam's voice was so deep it rumbled like thunder.

"That's right, it was Nakhimov, Mr. Nakhimov."

Hubble looked delighted that he'd been reminded of the name. "Generally speaking, I got nothing at all against coves with foreign-sounding names, nothing at all...but when Josie told me your Mr. Nakhimov was a *Russian*, well, let me tell you, that changed my opinion of him somewhat. A Russian, I said myself, what's a *Russian* doing having discussions about deliveries at a time like this?

"I may not be a educated man, Mr. Carter Bland, but I know treachery and I know treason when I see it, and having dealings with a man who, so I'm reliably informed by those what knows about such things, is more than likely related to a Russian admiral is just that! When yer at *war* you don't go doing business with the enemy, you call the authorities and have him put behind bars! Good English men are dying in the Crimea, and good English women, like that Florence Nightingale, are out there trying to save them, while you're up to your dastardly tricks." Hubble sat back in the chair, smiling. "And we have the papers to prove it – what d'you say to that?"

"How..." Bland winced, looking like he might actually have bitten his tongue in an effort to keep the word in his mouth. "I've no idea who or what you are talking about, sir – and who are *you* to talk to *me* about kidnap?" He glanced down at the massive arm holding him tight around the chest. "Unhand me this minute or..."

"Or what, Mr. Bland? Shall *I* tell *you* what's going to happen – which it will, a'coz I don't make idle threats? Instead of you dancing the Newgate hornpipe, hung till the last kick like what you ought to be, instead of that you'll be going to sea, my friend, for a very long time."

"To sea?" Bland frantically strained to free himself.

Hubble nodded. "I have friends downstairs this very minute, waiting to take you to the Port of London. You sail for the Antipodes on the next tide, Mr. Bland."

Josie slipped along the corridor and past the door leading down to the kitchens, holding her skirts up so she made as little noise as possible. Sounds and smells of cooking came from down below, but there was no sign of Tye Brookes.

"We're going to take the servants' stairs up to the second floor...if we see anyone, let me do the speaking." Tom made a *la-di-da!* face at Daniel who sniggered in reply; Josie raised one very stern eyebrow. "Less of that, you two!"

Grinning at each other, Daniel and Tom followed Josie up the stairs, mimicking the dainty way she walked, both too excited to be scared by what they were doing. For Daniel there was also the relief that he was no longer alone, that soon he'd be with Mr. Hubble and not long after that back with the rest of the circus, where he belonged.

Daniel looked at Tom, tiptoeing exaggeratedly beside him, with not a care in the world. Creeping around inside houses that belonged to other people was all in a day's work for him and Daniel felt sure Tom wasn't nervous in any way at all. Tom, he was also sure, would go back to his own life and probably forget all about the time he'd spent with the boy from the circus.

Just ahead, halfway up the next flight of stairs, Josie stopped and listened to see if she could hear anything; Daniel failed to notice and stumbled into her skirts, causing Tom to snort with laughter.

"*Stop playing the fool – this is serious!*" Josie whispered over her shoulder as she began walking again.

"I should say it is, my dear..." said a woman's voice that had a mean, rather acid sneer to it. "I hadn't thought to see *you* here again, except if you were dragged back like the common thief you are."

Daniel and Tom froze, while Josie slowly turned round to face the woman behind them.

"Queenie..." She muttered the word under her breath, as she saw Carter Bland's mother Renée, dressed all in black with a white lace shawl, standing in the doorway which led onto the first floor. Josie's finger tightened on the trigger of her Derringer...and then she noticed the rather larger pistol that was pointing right back at her. It was the oddest sight, this quite stout, not very tall old lady, piercing blue hawk-like eyes fixed on her victims, holding in her right hand not an ivory and lace fan, like you might expect, but a revolver. And holding it steady as a rock.

"Throw the little plaything down here, Miss Finnister." Renée Bland's mouth pursed in a humourless smile.

Before Josie could even think about doing what she'd been told to do, Tom Ducato did exactly as he'd been told and ran like Hell; he launched himself past Josie and disappeared up the stairs, grabbing her Derringer as he went. One moment he was there, the next he was gone, nimble as a mountain goat. Daniel looked at Josie, seeing an expression of complete surprise on her face that had to be the mirror of his own. While he might have a talent for doing tricks in the circus ring, when it came to looking after himself, Tom was certainly the master. He'd not only got away, he'd also taken the means to defend himself. If anyone was going to get out of this place unscathed, Daniel bet it would be Little Duke.

*"Let the child go, Queenie…"*

As he looked back down at the old lady, Daniel thought he could hear a noise from up above on the next floor, and wondered if it was Tom on the way to making good his escape. A bit of him wished he'd had the wit to run with him, but that would have left Josie to face this Queenie person on her own. Whoever she was and whatever she was planning on doing. To his astonishment what she did was come across the landing, almost as if she were gliding on wheels, and grab him by the wrist, her slightly chubby hand gripping like a vice.

"Is this the boy those fools my son hired let go, or was that the other one, with the springs in his heels?"

Josie, for once in her life, was lost for words – should she lie? Would Queenie hurt Daniel if she told the truth?

"Don't ever play poker, Miss Finnister." Renée smiled, slightly more genuinely this time, and pulled Daniel over to her. "Your face is an open book. Now come with me, I fear Carter may be in need of some assistance and you two might well be the trump card that wins this game." With the barrel of her pistol she indicated she wanted Josie to come down to the landing.

"Let the child go, Queenie...this is nothing at all to do with him. Nothing. And I don't want him hurt."

"Shouldn't have brought the filthy little wretch with you then, should you?" Renée stepped back to let Josie go in front of her. "Go through into the corridor and turn left, then walk slowly back down to the main staircase – and you, child," she yanked Daniel's wrist, "do as you are told and maybe Miss Finnister shall have her wish and her precious urchin won't get hurt..."

# CHAPTER 23
# LIFTING THE VEIL

A few steps down the corridor Daniel felt it happening again.

His eyelids fluttered, his vision blurred and he was aware of the strange prickling sensation – not hot, not cold either – crawling up from where the old woman was holding him, making its way all over every part of his body. Somewhere outside of him he could hear voices, hear his name being called by someone he thought he recognized, and another voice demanding to know what he was doing. Daniel closed his eyes for a moment, knowing by now that there was nothing he could do to stop this. And then he opened them...

*...it was night. Outside the room a storm howled like a pack of feral dogs driven wild by the scent of blood, rain hammering at the windows as if desperate to get in and the wind whistling at a pitch almost too high to hear. Curtains fought with the draughts and candles guttered, casting a sallow, wavering light on the scene unfolding within the four walls.*

*On a wide four-poster bed a woman lay in the grip of childbirth, one moment screaming like the storm outside, the next slumped, bathed in sweat on her pillows. Around her busied a younger woman, mopping her brow, offering her sips of gin and water and brandy, checking the progress this, the older woman's seventh child, was making into the world to join its three surviving brothers.*

*The door to the room opened as the mother-to-be lurched upwards, spitting out small blasphemies as she was taken by another stab of primal agony. A young girl came in carrying a large china jug; putting it on a table she stood back, eyes wide and watching everything that was happening.*

*"Nearly over now, Queenie...nearly over," the woman standing by the bed said.*

*"This labour will be the death of me, Alice...I'm too old for having a child, but that husband wants another boy, even if it puts me in the ground!" Renée Bland lay back, her blue eyes narrowed; she waved Alice to come to her. "But I shall not let him...have you done what I asked, Alice?"*

*"She's here." Alice nodded at the girl who had brought the jug in. "It's the new girl, what's just up from the country. If the Fates give you a boy, she'll take the mite and do away with him. You'll be rid of him for good."*

*"Are you sure, Alice? I am* not *having Elliot Bland getting his seventh son!" Whispering, Renée pulled Alice closer to her. "If it's a boy that superstitious old Irish goat will believe him to be magical and blessed, Alice...believe me, he will! The child will be everything to him, I know it, and my darling, darling Carter will get next to nothing or worse!"*

*"The girl will do it." Alice glanced over her shoulder. "For the purse you're offering I'm sure of that."*

*"Where is Elliot?"*

*"Downstairs, wetting the baby's head even before it's born."*

*"The drunker the better, if I have to tell him his boy was stillborn and so deformed I daredn't show him...*

*so ugly that one of the girls ran away when she saw the child and hasn't been seen since." Renée stiffened, a low groan deep in her chest building to a shriek, all but drowned out by a clap of thunder, as she was racked by a pain she'd forgotten it was possible to experience and survive.*

*The girl rushed forward. "I can see its head, Miss Alice, ma'am!*

*Then, as can be the way of these things, it was over. The child was born, bloody and mewling and having its cord tied.*

*"What is it?" whispered Renée.*

*"A boy," Alice replied, glancing at the girl; she reached into her apron pocket and brought out a small pouch which she dropped on the bed. There was a dull clink, like only gold coins make. "Swaddle the child, girl, take your sovs and be gone."*

*"What colour is his hair, Alice?"*

*"Black, what there is of it."*

*"His father's son."*

*"D'you want to see him?"*

*"No." Renée curled up on the bed, hair matted with sweat, dark circles under her eyes. "I want a brandy."*

*Alice watched as the girl wrapped the boy-child tightly in cloth in a strangely gentle way, considering what she was being paid to do with it, took the leather money pouch and left the room. In the silence left behind as the storm dropped for a moment, she looked over at the woman on the bed. "What was he going to be called, Renée?"*

*"Who?"*

*"The boy, what was Elliot going to call him?"*

*"Jack...he was to be called Jack."*

Daniel felt himself being shaken, heard his name being called and he found himself standing in a wide, brightly lit corridor, staring up at a face he recognized, but exactly why this was so he couldn't quite bring to mind. Behind the white-haired lady he saw Josie, staring at him as if he'd gone mad, then he looked back at the old woman and he remembered everything that'd happened.

This time he hadn't seen his future, he'd seen his past.

Queenie. The woman had called the one giving birth "Queenie", just like Josie had called the old lady. And what was it that Old Meggy had mumbled? He'd thought she was fuzzy in the head when she'd muttered something about his mother being a queen...then Daniel remembered the sovereign that Hannah had found when she'd unwrapped the swaddling cloth. *"Take your sovs and go..."* the woman called Alice had said to the young girl.

It was like finding the key to a door he'd never been able to open: it all made sense. He took a deep breath and looked straight up at Renée Bland. "I'm Jack, Mother, come to see you."

Renée Bland flinched, gaping at Daniel open-mouthed, her iron poise shaken. "What did you say, child?"

"Are you all right, Daniel?" Josie started towards him.

Renée waved her pistol in Josie's direction. "Stay away from him!" she hissed. "He's the spawn of the very Devil himself!"

"I am Jack, Mother."

"Don't say that, you wicked little imp!" Renée turned the gun on Daniel and held it with both hands. "I won't listen to this...this *vile*, sacrilegious talk, I won't!"

"You paid that girl, gave her gold to do away with me, Mother..."

"Silence, child!"

"But he says he's your child, Queenie." Josie, her mind racing as she tried to make sense of what was happening, moved more slowly towards Daniel this time. "What does he mean?"

"Nothing..." the gun barrel was shaking, "...he means nothing."

"He's an orphan, you know, just recently turned

twelve years old...wasn't that how long ago your last was born, Queenie?"

In the silence the pistol began to shake even more.

"I remember that particularly because it was soon after my father died, and I was made to work in The Sun...work for Carter, in the very tavern he stole from my old man." Above her Josie could hear footsteps, but Queenie, mesmerized by Daniel, didn't appear to have noticed.

"This has *nothing* to do with Carter..."

"I remember the talk, Queenie...about how much Elliot Bland wanted another boy, so the child would be a seventh son of a seventh son. That's what they said. And then the poor mite died, although they also said that it was a mercy he did, being as how he had a face like one of them gargoyles you see in churches."

Renée Bland remained pale and silent, the gun now pointing at the floor; her breath was coming in short gasps as her gaze remained fixed on the ragamuffin boy standing in front of her.

"That must've been a terrible thing, Queenie, to bear a child what dies. He'd have been the age of young Daniel here, *if* he'd lived...your Elliot, poor man, must've taken it something awful when he heard it was a boy you'd had, him wanting a seventh son so bad. I heard he believed the child would have had the gift of second sight...you know, be able to see things?" Josie looked over at Daniel. "Can you see things, Daniel?"

Daniel's heart was thumping, his stomach fluttered and he was shivering, even though it wasn't cold; he blinked and looked back at Josie, nodding. "Yes, I can."

"Don't lie, you evil, *evil* child!" Her eyes wide, lips stretched back over yellowed teeth, Renée Bland brought the pistol back up. "Liars don't go to Heaven when they die..."

"No, Queenie!" Josie screamed as the old lady pulled the trigger, diving at her and sending the two of them sprawling onto the floor, while the shot went wild and hit the ceiling. The pistol flew from Renée Bland's hands, skittering away down the corridor.

With the sound of the gunshot still echoing in his ears and the hot smell of cordite burning his nostrils, Daniel stood rooted to the spot. It *had* to be true, the woman Josie called Queenie *was* his mother! And the gold sovereign. Hannah said she'd found it in his hand when they'd unwrapped the cloth he'd been swaddled in, and had kept it safe because, she said, it was the only link with his past. The very link which had connected him to the scene he'd witnessed just now when Renée Bland had grabbed him by the wrist.

It *had* to be true.

Why the girl had saved his life instead of ending it he

had no idea. He didn't know how to feel. He'd done the very thing that every orphan dreams of doing: he'd found his mother. But his was a mother who had never wanted him in the first place, who had tried to kill him not once, but twice. This was not how he had always imagined it would be, and he'd imagined it many times; in his mind's eye his mother, who'd been searching for him since the day he'd been stolen from her, would see him on Savage in the circus ring and know, just *know* he was her child. She would not try and shoot him dead.

Daniel realized he could hear shouting and running feet, and then, lumbering round the corner into the corridor, gun in hand, he saw the awesome sight of Mr. Hubble come roaring into view, closely followed by Sam Baston. The old boxer stopped dead in his tracks at what he saw in front of him – which was Josie, who he thought was tucked safely away in Mrs. Scott's, picking herself up from beside the figure of an old lady on the floor, and Daniel...Daniel who was supposed to be lost somewhere in the back alleys of London, but was standing right in front of him, and who he barely recognized because he looked like he'd slept in a sty. And on the carpet by his feet there was a pistol, a wisp of smoke coming out of its barrel.

"Daniel?" Mr. Hubble walked forward a couple of steps, his arms outstretched, and Daniel ran to him, never so glad to see anyone in his life. "Are you all right, boy?"

"I am…I am, sir." Daniel stood very close to the big man, who rested his huge, scarred hand protectively on his shoulder.

They looked, thought Josie as she brushed herself down, like a bear and his cub. And you had to be careful with bears, especially angry ones.

"What the blue blazes," Hubble growled, "is going on here, Josie Finnister?"

# CHAPTER 24
# SKIN OF THE TEETH

Before Josie had a chance to reply there was the sound from downstairs of someone giving a brass door knocker a good pounding. Everyone stood and waited for what would happen next, their concentration broken by Renée Bland groaning and trying to get up off the floor.

"It's the rozzers, Bruise!" said a voice from downstairs. "Someone must've told 'em about the gunshots. What now?"

Hubble bent down and picked up the pistol. "Like as not they're just at the front, come to see what's up. Josie, take Daniel down the back stairs – Sam, go with them. Me and the rest of the boys'll join you in a minute or two."

As Josie hustled Daniel back out of the corridor he glanced back and saw the old woman who'd given birth to him, and then discarded him like an unwanted gift, staring at him, a strange, almost pleading look in her eyes. But, looking at her, he realized he felt nothing. He'd found his mother, he'd met a brother – like he'd always dreamed of doing – and they neither of them were what he'd imagined or thought he deserved as a family. He turned and walked away. Sam Baston came striding after them and, as he ducked to come through the door, Daniel saw the legs of the person he had slung over his right shoulder.

"Good ta see ya, Daniel." Sam grinned. "Ya look a mess, boy!"

"Come on – no time for catch-up now!" Josie was already halfway down to the next landing.

Walking hurriedly along the narrow passageway to the back entrance, they went past the stairs which led to the kitchens and cellars, and as they did so a couple of sweat-stained faces peered round the doorway. "What's going on up here?" a bearded man called after them.

"Cook thought he hear'd something, and sent us to find out..." The second man stopped mid-sentence. "'Ere, is that Mr. Bland you got there?"

Daniel looked back at the figure Sam was carrying and saw him try to lash out with his legs. Without breaking his stride Sam casually banged the man's head on the wall, and the kicking and grunting stopped.

The bearded man cackled, revealing a brown, snaggled graveyard of teeth, and nudged his friend in the ribs. "Good riddance to 'im, I say!"

Once outside they went and stood by the gate to the wide back alley and waited in the dark. Curious, Daniel looked at the semi-conscious Carter Bland, mouth gagged, hair in disarray, his fancy cravat hanging loose. His brother. He'd always wondered about whether he had brothers or sisters, had thought how marvellous it would be to meet them and become their friends, as you surely must with your own family. Maybe they wouldn't all be as bad as Carter and his mother, but Daniel would be quite happy if he never found out. From behind them came a thundering of boots, first on floorboards and then on stone paving, and moments later Mr. Hubble and four other men had joined them by the gate.

"Change of plan..." Hubble wheezed, catching his breath; he hadn't run this much in donkey's years. "Tye, Walt, them growlers what were going to pick us up at the front, nip as fast as you like to where they're waiting and make sure they stay there. We'll come and meet you."

Daniel watched the two men run off into the night, and as the rest of the group followed after them he heard a commotion somewhere inside The Ace, the sound of shouting and doors banging and clomping feet. It sounded like someone had opened up and let the police in.

"Kit," Hubble had his breath back now, "take the rear and shoot over the heads of anyone what's coming after us… Henry, put your gun away and scout the front like you was out for a stroll. Whistle us if you see any bobbies."

The next few minutes stretched out like hours as this odd collection of friends and one foe made their way as fast as they could, from shadow to shadow, to the side street where Hubble had paid two cabs to wait until called for. Somewhere up ahead a bird warbled, strangely for the time of day, a blackbird, and Hubble abruptly stopped walking, waving for everyone to do the same.

Creeping forward, Hubble flattened his not inconsiderable bulk against the wall of a house and peered round the corner. As he did Daniel heard the slap of reins, and voices chivvying horses to move on.

"The bobby's walking off, they're coming to get us," Hubble whispered over his shoulder, and everyone let out a sigh of relief.

The second growler pulled away from the kerb, the clip-clop of the horse's hooves echoing in the quiet. Minutes before, the other cab had left, taking Kit Pullman and Henry Grey, along with their reluctant passenger, to the docks where the schooner *Regis Sound* was waiting to leave; ahead of her crew was a journey that wouldn't see the swift two-master back in her home port for two good years or more.

Sitting opposite Josie and Sam Baston, and next to Mr. Hubble, who had a protective arm round his shoulder, Daniel looked out of the cab's window; he felt empty...lost and found at the same time. He was, despite having discovered his mother, as much of an orphan as he'd always been and almost the worse off for knowing the truth.

The feeling of isolation and loss for some reason reminded him of Tom, and his thoughts turned to wondering what had happened to the Little Duke. He guessed he'd probably be all right. That boy was a survivor, and he'd likely get good money from Old Meggy for Josie's little pistol.

Daniel turned away from the window and thought

about the man he now knew was his brother. "What's going to happen to Mr. Bland?"

Hubble thought for a moment. "Nothing less than he deserves, eh, Josie?"

Josie looked up from staring at a sheaf of folded papers on her lap, all tied up in red ribbon and sealed with wax. "Only if he never comes back, Bruise." She looked down at the papers again, touching them as if she could hardly believe they were there, which in truth she couldn't. "How did you get these?"

"The title to The Sun? Sam wrung it out of Mr. Bland. Didn't take long for him to squeal and tell where he kept it." Hubble smiled and patted Daniel's shoulder. "What is it they say? Possession's the thing what counts when it comes to the law? Something like that, I'm sure...main thing is, you have it back now and the tavern's yours again, my girl."

"What if he does come back?" Daniel frowned.

"That ain't a likely proposition, in my view, as I told him that the papers what Josie took, the ones proving he's been dealing with the Russians and should be up for treason, would be delivered into the right hands in Whitehall the very first thing tomorrow. If Carter Bland shows his face in these latitudes again I'll warrant he'll find he's looking straight at a firing squad."

"And me?" Daniel looked uneasy, almost nervous.

"You, lad? What about you?"

Josie cleared her throat and smiled at Daniel, guessing the boy did not want to go into too much detail about what had happened, but that he needed to say something. "He found out something, Bruise... something what explains a lot of things."

"And that might be?" Hubble turned to Daniel.

"Queenie was his mother..."

Hubble looked back at Josie, lifted his hand as if he was about to say something, stopped, frowned and then started again. "That old lady with the pistol, what you floored? Renée Bland is his mother?" Josie nodded. "*She's* the one left him with us that godforsaken night?"

"No, she paid some skivvy girl to do her dirty work and get rid of him for her. Queenie wanted him dead."

"What kind of heathen woman would do a thing like that?"

"Folk do it all tha time, Bruise, get rid of the child they don' want." Sam Baston shrugged. "Sad to say, but true, not every woman make a mother."

"But *why* did she do it?"

Josie glanced at Daniel, his dirty, puzzled face sad and downcast, and her heart went out to him, this boy who must be wondering why his mother couldn't have loved him and kept him. She shook her head very slightly, as if to say "not now". "She had her own bad reasons, Bruise."

Hubble's great paw of a hand hugged Daniel's shoulder. "It's an ill wind, boy."

Daniel nodded, leaning against the big man. His head was full of a confusion of thoughts, but he was sure he understood what Mr. Hubble meant. Although he had now, truly, lost his mother, she was a woman who had never wanted him anyway. Truth was, though, he'd always had a family, the one he'd got the night he'd been abandoned, another kind of family all together. And, as Mr. Hubble always said, fair exchange was no robbery.

The cab turned off into a smaller street and pulled up next to a nondescript building. Sam opened the door and got out, followed by Josie. Daniel hung back as Mr. Hubble got up.

"What is it?"

Daniel looked away. "Nothing..."

"Don't believe that for a moment."

"It's just..." Daniel took a deep breath and then the question tumbled out. "I'm not that woman's son, am I, not really – this doesn't change anything, does it?"

"You never were hers, Daniel, son. Never." Mr. Hubble gathered Daniel even closer to him. "You came to us as a child not even a day old, you've become the boy you are with us, and I hope you will stay to become the man. None of this don't change a thing, boy, and you don't *never* have to think like that – you're Daniel Hubble, and I'll thump into kingdom come anyone who says different!"

# Epilogue

Little Duke opened the door at the top of the stairs, crept out into an empty corridor and closed it carefully behind him. To his right, a few yards away, was another door, although this one looked like it had been opened by a cannonball. But an open door was an open door and an opportunity you didn't pass up, not if you wanted to eat.

Tiptoeing over to it, Tom Ducato stopped and listened. He could hear voices, not in the room the broken door let on to, but nearby; someone was whining and complaining, someone else's gravel tones were asking questions, although he couldn't quite make out what either was saying. Careful to be as quiet as possible, Tom slipped into the room and stood still, looking round to try and get his bearings. As he saw where he was he stared as if his eyes were out on stalks. Because he was in the fanciest, most elaborate room he'd ever seen in his whole life. He'd never believed it when he'd heard people talk of places which had silk on the walls and crystal chandeliers like glass fountains of light and chairs which truly looked like they were fit for kings to sit on. And here he was, as he lived and breathed, actually standing in one.

He was brought out of his reverie by the sound of yelling and scuffling.

"Tell me where it is, right now, else I'll have him crack your ribs, so help me," said the gruff voice.

"You can't..." the whiny voice screamed, then sobbed, "...all right, all right! It's in the desk...third drawer down on the left."

Tom moved further into the room, making his way over to where he could stand behind the door and look through the gap into where the other people were. Standing there he could hear and not be seen.

"Well, bless me, Mr. Bland, so you *were* telling the

truth!" The man with the gruff voice chuckled. "Josie will be pleased to have these back."

"You can't do this!" the other man griped like a spoiled child.

"Unfortunately for you, Mr. Bland, that ain't so..."

Tom tried looking through the tiny gap between the door and the jamb and could just make out a large man with the battered face of someone used to settling arguments with his fists. Tom saw the man push himself up out of the chair he was sitting in and disappear from view.

"...time to go, Sam. Tie Mr. Bland up and stuff something in his pie-hole to keep him quiet – he has an appointment to keep at the docks."

Quiet as a mouse, Tom moved away from the door and behind one of the high-backed, fabric-covered chairs. He reckoned he'd be completely hidden if they came out this way, and a few minutes later he was proved correct.

As soon as the two men had left, one of them with a third person slung over his shoulder, Tom was up and into the room they'd come out of. He stood for a moment, rubbing his hands together and thinking about what to do next. This had to be done quickly, he knew, but it must also be done properly as, for a boy like him, this was a once-in-a-lifetime chance.

He went straight over to the desk. Here, from what he'd overheard, was where the whining man obviously kept his valuable things. With his hands and his eyes Tom began searching, all the while listening as he'd never listened before for any sound that might signal trouble was coming his way. He had only just started going through the second drawer when he heard the pistol shot from, it sounded like, the floor below; *Don't rush, and don't panic!* he kept reminding himself. *Make every second count.*

By the time he'd been through the six side drawers he'd found some gold and pearl cufflinks, a pair of gold-framed reading glasses and a diamond-tipped silver toothpick, nothing to complain about, but nowhere near the haul he'd hoped for. As he pulled out the central drawer and put it on the desk in front of him, like Old Meggy had taught him to do, his spirits lifted. Like she said, if you don't take it all out, you don't know what all's in there. And she was right, because there it was, at the back, a "secret" compartment.

Tom opened it, not knowing what to expect, and found a key. He'd seen keys just like this before and he knew exactly what he must do next: find the safe that it opened. Painfully aware the sands must be running out (he could hear distant voices and movement, none of it yet coming his way) he looked around the room. He'd listened to the cracksmen and burglars talking amongst themselves late at night in the taverns, after they'd finished their work, of where people thought it best to hide things. Safes, he remembered, were often put behind pictures.

A couple of minutes later Tom had discovered it wasn't true of this particular room, but then he spotted the small wooden cabinet decorated with delicate wooden inlay. It was squat, it looked heavy and it was the size you might expect a safe to be. He went over to it and opened the door to reveal a black metal box with a brass label on it.

Kneeling down Tom unlocked the safe and pulled open the door. In the small interior compartment, almost hidden by a pile of leather-bound books, he saw a black velvet pouch with a gold crest embroidered on it, an eagle with two heads, each wearing a crown, with its wings outstretched; he reached in and picked it up. The velvet was the softest thing he'd ever touched. The pouch had weight, but not much, and felt as if it contained a number of quite small things. He pulled open the top and poured the contents into the palm of his hand. Diamonds! A *fortune* in diamonds, all sparkling with an icy fire in the light.

"So," Tom muttered to himself as he wondered if a

quick exit down the drainpipe might not be the best way out of this place, "Danny-boy wasn't making it up after all..."

## THE END

**GRAHAM MARKS** had his first book of poetry published while he was at art school, studying graphic design. After a successful career as an art director he decided it was time for a change and now works as a journalist and author. He has written everything from comic strips and film tie-ins to advertising copy and novels, and he has most recently been highly acclaimed for his Young Adult books. *Snatched!* is his first historical novel.

When he's not writing books, Graham is writing about them as the Children's Editor for Publishing News. He's married to fellow journalist and author Nadia Marks, and lives in London with his two sons and a cat called Boots.

Find out more about Graham Marks at
www.marksworks.co.uk

# THE FANTASTICAL ADVENTURES OF THE INVISIBLE BOY

## LLOYD ALEXANDER

David hates being The Invisible Boy, ignored by his eccentric family because he's considered too young to understand anything. But right now he's happy to be forgotten. Signed off school to recover from a bout of pneumonia, David is looking forward to plenty of time for his imaginary swashbuckling adventures as The Sea-Fox, buccaneer captain and terror of the sea lanes.Then his dry-as-dust aunt volunteers as his tutor and David is devastated. This is worse than school! But it turns out that Aunt Annie has some secrets to share, and together they set off on an exciting fantastical voyage.

"This book is delightful, a warm homage to creativity and the power of imagination." *TES Teacher*

An ALA Notable Book

A *School Library Journal* Best Book of the Year

0 7460 6041 6

# The Shadow Garden

## Andrew Matthews

Matty's sixth sense tells her that Tagram House is harbouring a dark secret. The master, Dr. Hobbes, seems charming on the surface but underneath Matty detects a glint of razor-sharp steel. Her fears lead Matty to the eerie Shadow Garden, and she eventually discovers what's buried there. Now she must untangle the mystery before disaster engulfs everyone.

Like cold fingers reaching from the grave, a chilling atmosphere of mystery and suspense seeps through the pages of this haunting ghost story.

"This is a highly atmospheric novel...a satisfying, gripping read with a truly alarming climax." *School Librarian*

0 7460 6794 1

# THE HISTORICAL HOUSE

"Historically strong, these are also dramatic stories with a real sense of atmosphere." *The Guardian*

## LIZZIE'S WISH
## ADÈLE GERAS

Struggling to adapt to a new life in London, Lizzie looks forward to her mother's letters from home. When the letters suddenly stop, Lizzie sets out to discover the truth and finds herself on a rescue mission.

0 7460 6030 0

## POLLY'S MARCH
## LINDA NEWBERY

When Polly discovers that her new neighbours are suffragettes she is intrigued and becomes determined to join their protest march. But will she risk the disapproval of her parents and do what she thinks is right?

0 7460 6031 9

## JOSIE UNDER FIRE
## ANN TURNBULL

Josie wants to fit in with her cousin Edith's friends, playing on bombsites and teasing a timid classmate. But when the bullying gets out of hand, will she risk revealing her own secret to make a stand?

0 7460 6032 7